THE VALKYRIE'S RULE

BOOK 2: THE VALKYRIE OF BIRCA

TANYA NELLESTEIN

wine&words

First Edition June 2021
Editing by Kelly Rigby
www.writewithkelly.com

Cover design by Jacqueline Hayley
www.jacquelinehayley.com

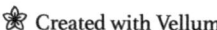 Created with Vellum

For Olivia,
the fiercest shield maiden I know.

PROLOGUE

*T*ingvalla - after the death of Sigurd the Black

Audolf Olvirsson spat onto the sand and watched as the royal party made their way down the docks. Sigurd's displaced army followed closely behind like the fools they were. Blonde hair spilled over the black fur that had, until this morning, adorned the shoulders of Sigurd the Black. His shield was strapped to her back; his spear clasped in her hand. None of Sigurd's weapons had been left with his body; ensuring he would receive no passage to Valhalla.

"Níðingr!" He spat on the ground once more, punctuating his hatred of her.

From Audolf's position on the bank of the fjord, he watched them make ready to sail back to Birca. As the woman stepped up onto the side of the waiting drakkar, she turned in his direction.

Even at this distance, Audolf could see the blood of Sigurd painted across her face. Her declaration of her deeds to men and the gods alike. It was a sentiment he did not share.

"Brenna of Birca, another will decide if you are worthy to carry the shield of Sigurd the Black." He spoke into the wind, hoping his words would carry to the drakkar and strike a warning to those abroad.

Audolf had no intention of pledging his fealty to King Aric or the so-called Valkyrie of Birca. Bloodlust fuelled his veins and their talk of peace bored him. Yet he'd stayed to hear what the King intended. It would be useful information when he returned to the only place he thought of as home: Gyldarhagi.

Audolf was one of the few to know the truth of Sigurd the Black's parentage. The man himself had not known who his father was, believing it to be some nameless karl who took his fill of a slave then left. Which was almost true... except it was not a nameless karl who fathered him. It was Gorm, the warmonger and self-proclaimed King of Gyldarhagi.

Sigurd may have been ruthless and bloody-minded, but there was something in him that made him weak. He craved acknowledgement. From a watchful distance, Gorm had recognised it and sent Audolf to keep an eye on his bastard son.

Audolf knew that despite never meeting or acknowledging Sigurd as his own flesh and blood, Gorm would want to know of his demise. He may want to take bloody revenge on the one who'd taken his life, reclaim Tingvalla and mayhap Birca for his own. And that would mean war and bloodshed. Two of Audolf's favourite things.

Grinning, he picked up his axe and shield. It was time to go home.

1

BIRCA AD - 821

For the second time that day, Brenna whispered a prayer of thanks to the gods for insisting weapons be left outside the great hall when the Ting was in session. Instead of actual bloodshed, she had only to contend with the elaborate descriptions of how Hjalmar Brynjarsson, formerly a soldier with Sigurd the Black's army, would gut not only the farmer, Vragi Ulfertsson, but his wife and three daughters, for bringing this matter before the Jarl and the Ting.

"Enough!" The edge to Brenna's voice quietened the feuding neighbours. "Hjalmar Brynjarsson, you have unlawfully laid claim to a parcel of land belonging to Vragi Ulfertsson. The land in question lies cleared and unplanted as it will form the dowry for Vragi's eldest daughter, Embla - it is not free for you to claim."

"Then I will claim the wench's hand in marriage!" boomed Hjalmar, his height amplifying his voice across the hall.

The girl's mother gasped, pulling Embla into her arms.

Murmurs of disgust from Birca's older residents interplayed with snorts of mirth from the newcomers.

Brenna held her hand up, quieting the outrage. "There will be no *claiming* of any person in this town."

"Embla?" She turned to the girl, her face as white as snow under her dark tresses. "What say you? Do you wish to marry Hjalmar Brynjarsson?"

Trembling in her mother's arms, her eyes wide with fear, Embla shook her head. "Nei, I do not," she whispered.

"Then it is settled - your proposal is rejected." Brenna's contempt for the suggestion dripped from every word.

"Then I will claim his next daughter," said Hjalmar, to the roar of laughter from his former comrades in arms.

"By Thor's hammer, you make a mockery of this coun-cil!" Ivar of Bulandshofoi rose from his seat. "The invitation by which you are here can just as easily be retracted."

Brenna suppressed the low rumble in the back of her throat at the audacity of the fífl. She was, however, grateful for Ivar's loyalty. Once a hersir in Sigurd's army, Ivar had become an important adviser. A bridge between the men he once commanded under Sigurd, and Brenna's warriors of Birca.

"What are we to do, Ivar?" growled Hjalmar. "How are we to live if we cannot farm the land? Jarl Brenna," he spat the words and looked pointedly at Brenna, "has forbidden us to go raiding."

Brenna refused to return his look, even as agreement rose from around the hall. Merriment quickly turning to frustrated anger.

Her own anger simmered; could they not see what she was trying to achieve for all of them? Standing between the lands of the Vikings and the Baltic trade routes, Birca was perfectly positioned to become the greatest trade centre in all of Midgard. Any day now, she expected Vali to return with new trade agreements from the East.

"You would have the future of this town and its people put in jeopardy so a few of you can go raiding?" Brenna's voice was steel. She looked out across the great hall into a sea of disapproval. Warriors, new and old were crowded into every available space, along with a dozen or so farmers.

Allowing raiding parties to depart from her shores would not win them any favour across the seas. Even King Aric had forbidden any raiding in the East, sending his longboats to the West.

"You have come here as warriors. You should be keeping up with your training and maintaining the armoury." The ongoing complaints from all factions within Birca had worn Brenna's patience thin. "You must learn to fight with Birca's army. Learn to become one so no army can defeat us."

"What army would be foolish enough to face the Valkyrie of Birca?" Sarcasm dripped from Hjalmar's words.

His words landed as bitingly as a slap to her face. Slowly, Brenna rose to her feet.

All her life she had believed it was her fate to rule; to lead. The Seer had told her this was the will of the gods when she was a mere child at play. Her own belief and determination had brought her to this place where she now stood as the Jarl of Birca. But lately she wondered, what did she know of leadership?

"I have made no secret of the way in which I chose to rule here in Birca, and it is not through pillage and plun-der." Her voice rang out, strong and steady across the great hall. "It is my desire and, I believe, the will of the gods that Birca prospers through trade and growth, not war and raiding."

Her skin prickled with the eyes of her council upon her.

This group of men had advised and supported her late husband when he had been the Jarl of Birca. They had always had so much to say and debate when Tarben sat on the high chair. Now, they listened and nodded as she spoke, contributing little. Where once they were sources of wisdom and active support, now they were effectively invisible. Brenna knew they may not oppose her, but they did not stand with her either.

Gita believed it was because the council were afraid. That to anger Brenna would invoke the wrath of the gods - and they too would find their throats slit as they lay in their beds. Brenna had laughed at the serving girl's words. She would no sooner find her way to the bedchambers of her councilmen than she would order their deaths. Surely, they could not fear their Jarl? But mayhap, there was some merit to her argument?

"You are the Valkyrie of Birca. Anointed as Jarl by the gods to rule." Gita had reminded her. "You are loved, it is true, but you are also feared. These men have naught seen the likes of you before."

"Their silent agreement hinders more than helps. Surely, they see I need their counsel, just as Jarl Beinersson did?" Brenna argued.

"Jarl Beinersson could not see the gift the gods bestowed on him in making you his wife. He fell in battle, a noble warrior, but unable to save his people. You were the one to do that."

Brenna's skill with her sword and axe was mayhap her greatest strength. But it was not a strength that served her well in present circumstances. Without a war, the council seemed to merely tolerate her. If it wasn't for Ivar, she wouldn't know who to trust.

Brenna did not search for Gita in the great hall as she

faced her people. It would not do for the Jarl of Birca to look to her maid for support. She was grateful for Ivar's steady presence at her side, he knew Sigurd's followers well and he understood the difficulty of her current position. She needed warriors to defend the town and her people; however, what was she to do with an army that had no battle to fight?

She took a deep breath. She was the Jarl, she must take control of this situation. Brenna narrowed her gaze on Hjalmar Brynjarsson.

"The foolish will always find a reason to fight," she continued. She took a step forward on the dais. "If you choose to live in Birca, you will be under the protection of Birca. We must always be prepared, and I've no desire to face an enemy with an army of fools."

Hjalmar snarled but held his tongue.

"Lodgings and food are provided for the warriors of Birca. What need have you for another man's land?"

Hjalmar jutted his chin out, the challenge clear in his battle worn features. "Jarl, if I am to call Birca home, I must have something more to offer than my sword."

Brenna clenched her fists by her side. "You think stolen land will win you a wife?"

Snickers echoed around the hall.

"Honour will win me a wife, Jarl." Hjalmar's eyes flashed with anger. "Where is the honour in doing nothing? Owning nothing? How could I provide for a wife when I have no means with which to do so?"

Her conscience poked at her. Was this not a similar line of reasoning that had dissuaded her from marrying Vali? She raised her chin as if her stature could ward off these men's criticisms - and her own internal chastisement.

"We have no land to farm, naught to trade and you

forbade us from raiding?" called another voice from the crowd.

"The few coins you throw at our feet are only enough to keep the alehouses open," yelled another.

"The Jarl is more than generous with you rassragrs," snarled Vragi, turning to face the other man.

"*Rassragr?*" Hjalmar launched himself at Vragi and the hall erupted behind them.

"By the gods," muttered Ivar as fists flew in all directions. Skull cracked against skull. Women shielded their children, making for the door or taking cover against the walls.

"Odin, help me," said Brenna as her people turned on each other.

She stepped down from the dais, wading through the wrestling bodies, towards Hjalmar and Vragi. Blood covered their faces and their fists. Do these people lust for battle so much they would start a war in her hall? A blood curdling howl sounded from Vragi; his ear ripped from his head and held firm between Hjalmar's teeth. Brenna pulled them apart, calling for her guards to arrest them both.

The appearance of guards with shields and swords halted most of the fighting. Vragi continued to scream obscenities at Hjalmar, who began to chew the severed ear. Brenna's stomach turned a little and she was thankful when both men were dragged away.

Behind her, members of the council had risen and were taking their leave. Brenna bristled with frustration at their obvious aversion to lending support in case they might actually have to do something.

She straightened her spine. She was the Jarl and she would enforce her rule. With her people, and the council. Although, the gods knew how she craved just a moment of reprieve from duty; a moment in the arms of Vali.

"Jarl?"

A boy she recognised from the docks stood breathless at her side. She turned to give him her attention. "What is it, Ketil?"

"A drakkar has been spotted at the mouth of the fjord. Lord Vali approaches."

Vali, at last! It seemed the gods had heard her silent plea.

She searched for Ivar and found him separating the last of the men throwing fists.

"Ivar! Vali approaches. I will go to greet him." She headed for the door, stepping around benches that had been upended in the melee.

"Jarl, a word?"

She halted in her tracks, forcing patience despite her body's visceral need to be with Vali. "What is it, Ivar?"

The man drew himself up to his full height, bringing himself eye level with Brenna. Though what he lacked in height, he made up for in width and muscle.

"Forgive me, but I believe you must take swift action before unrest spreads throughout the entire village."

She looked around her, taking in the bloodied faces and disordered hall. The people of Birca had struggled to accept those responsible for so much death and bloodshed in Sigurd's assault on them. But these warriors had come to Birca on the strength of her word that they would bear no consequences for their past actions.

"Ivar, this is not a problem that can be solved in haste." She rested her hand on his shoulder. "The troublemakers have been secured and they would do well to reflect upon their actions."

The look of consternation on his face suggested he was not convinced. Regardless, Ivar, and the rest of Birca would have to wait.

"I will send for you when I am ready to discuss the matter further." She patted his shoulder before continuing on her way.

2

The silhouette of Birca against the late afternoon sun was a welcome sight across the fjord. Vali stood at the bow of his longboat, his anticipation building. The envoy had been a success, and not for the first time he marvelled at how little he missed his old life of raiding.

But he did miss Brenna.

It had been four long months since he'd laid eyes on her. He'd heard from various wanderers and traders that Birca had remained safe from attack in his absence, and he was sure she would have consolidated her position as Jarl. The people loved her. He loved her.

His smile stretched from ear to ear. Part of him hoped she'd not planned a feast for his return. He would much rather spend the evening in her bed than at her side in the great hall.

"I can only imagine what has put that smile on your face," said Frode, coming to join him at the bow. "Or should I say, *who* has put that smile on your face."

Vali slapped his friend on the back. "It will be good to be home."

"Home? Is that now Birca?"

"Home is where Brenna is." The words came easily and truthfully.

Frode gave him a good-natured shove. "Ah, I see how it is."

"Frode, will you even stay a night at Birca before going back to Fornsigtuna and your wife?"

"Ja, of course, Vali." Frode's face was a picture of outrage at his suggestion. Although the twinkle in his eye suggested there was something more to this. "What is one more day?"

Frode's lips twitched, despite his serious tone.

"A day is naught, I suppose," said Vali. "But what of the night?"

The twitch turned into a smile. "I will spend the night with my beautiful wife who, if the gods saw fit to accommodate our plans, should have arrived in Birca within this past week."

Vali laughed out loud. "I cannot imagine the gods would seek to keep young lovers apart longer than is necessary."

"What is true for me, is also true for you."

Vali looked across the water to Birca, and the woman who had held his heart for as long as he could remember. "Ja, so it would seem."

The two men stood shoulder to shoulder and watched Birca take shape as the longboat pulled closer. Buildings became more defined and in moments Vali would be able to make out the smoke lifting from the longhouses and people scurrying like ants as they went about their day.

"I have hope Nissa will not be waiting alone for me," said Frode.

Vali turned to look at his friend.

"It was early days, but Nissa was sure she was with child

before I departed on this journey." Frode's countenance was one of hope and barely concealed delight.

He slapped his friend on the back. "I am so happy for you, my friend," said Vali. "The gods truly bless you."

"Ja, they do."

Vali raised his face to catch the sun's warmth. A gentle breeze had picked up and quickened the pace of the drakkar as it sailed closer to its destination. The call of the horn had heralded their approach and a crowd now gathered at the dock. Vali turned his attention back to his crew, giving the order to make ready.

The longboat pulled into the port and many hands reached out to bring the vessel close. Vali leapt onto the dock as ropes were thrown out to tie the ship in place; Frode was only a step behind. Vali searched the faces for Brenna, knowing she would hardly wait for him with an armed guard or a dozen servants ready to do her bidding. She may be Jarl but she was not one for unnecessary pageantry.

"Frode!"

Vali glanced to his right and found his friend within the embrace of his wife. When he pulled back, Vali could see the roundness of Nissa's belly protruding from her over-dress. His heart swelled with happiness for his friends, as well as a twinge of jealousy.

Nei, Brenna was still a new Jarl. He must give her time.

Most of his crew had disembarked and those with family and friends present were being greeted. Others set about unloading the longboat. Vali had secured a number of samples of what was to come with his newly established trade agreements. But he cared naught for that now.

Where is Brenna? He had much to share with her. By the gods, he needed her smile; the one she saved only for him.

His eyes swept the dock and beyond, finally catching sight of a figure hurrying through the crowd.

Her blonde hair was braided back from her face, its length billowing behind her in contrast to the deep blue gown she wore. His heart skipped a beat, propelling him past the happy reunions of men and their families on the pier. Her smile burst across her face as he neared, her cheeks flushed and eyes shining. His own face split in two. Gods, how he'd missed her.

He slowed, expecting the Jarl, rather than his lover, to greet him in such a public place. As much as his body ached for her, he could wait to feel her in his arms until they were alone.

"Well m-" Her lips closed over his before he could get his greeting out.

She placed her hands on his chest, her fingers curling around the cloak that covered his shoulders. Her body pressing against his caused an immediate reaction.

His hands came up to her waist as the kiss deepened, his tongue entwining with hers. The sounds of the sea and land faded into nothing as he melted completely into her.

She pulled back a little. "Welcome home, Lord Vali," she whispered against his mouth.

"Jarl Brenna. " He dipped his forehead onto hers.

Straightening her shoulders, and his cloak, she took a step back. "Come, I am eager to hear of your journey." Her voice was all business, but the glint in her eye was pure mischief.

"Of course." He inclined his head to hide the desire in his eyes.

Linking her arm through his, Brenna steered them in the direction of the great hall, amidst the knowing grins and murmured greetings of his crew and their families. Vali was vaguely aware of the town as they made their way through. The marketplace was full of hustle and bustle, already grown so much larger than when he'd left. Children played under the feet of adults as they worked and wandered.

Three men leant against a pigpen. He could not hear what they were saying, but their heated stares in the direction of he and Brenna gave him pause.

"Do you know those men?" he asked.

Her sigh was barely audible. "They were at the Ting earlier. Mayhap they were stirred by Hjalmar Brynjarsson's words."

"Newcomers?" He raised an eyebrow in question. He didn't recognise the three men or the name Brenna had just mentioned. "Are they causing trouble?"

"Ja, newcomers," said Brenna, returning their stares as the two of them passed by. "They have grown restless without a battle to fight." She turned back to him, the smile not quite meeting her eyes this time. "But let's not discuss this now. Ivar and I will see to it later."

"You and Ivar? Not the council?" Had Ivar joined the council while he'd been travelling? His thoughts were interrupted by a more familiar face.

"Welcome home, Vali! Jarl Brenna."

He turned to find Snorri, one of Brenna's commanders, or hersirs, of her army. "Snorri! I hear you are well rested after this summer," he said with jest.

Snorri was tall and wiry, standing a head taller than most men. His shaved skull was covered with runes inked into his skin. "Ja, my wife has enjoyed putting me to work in the fields with a plough on my back."

"A harder task master than you, I'll bet."

The hardened warrior grinned. "That she is. But tell me, was your journey blessed by the gods?"

Vali nodded to Brenna. "I must speak with the Jarl first, of course. Let us say the gods continue to smile on our Jarl and Birca."

"Ah, that is good to hear. Jarl Brenna, I'm sure you are pleased to know at least one thing has gone to plan."

Vali frowned. What had not gone to plan? Brenna hadn't wanted to discuss what had happened at the Ting. Mayhap it was not an isolated incident? They said their farewells and continued on to the great hall. He shook the concern away, shifting his attention instead to Brenna explaining the changes they'd planned for the private quarters in the hall and how they'd been completed in his absence. He looked forward to seeing them for himself... eventually.

However, when he stepped inside the hall, he found the room in disarray. Fire burned low in the oblong fire pit in the centre of the room and he waited a moment for his eyes to adjust. The great hall was all but empty, save for servants sweeping out the floor and righting furniture.

"Brenna, what exactly-" Again, his question was interrupted.

"Lord Vali? You are returned." Gita made her way to him, gesturing for another servant to take his cloak.

"Well met, Gita. It's good to see you."

Gita had transformed in the last six months from a quiet serving girl to a confident woman, in charge of the Jarl's house and all her servants. Her clothes were new and clean, and her light brown hair neatly braided.

"You must be hungry. I will fix you some refreshment."

"Thank you, Gita." He peered at the signs of the fight that had occurred in the hall.

"Come, "said Brenna, taking his arm. "Let's not ruin your homecoming by discussing the petty arguments of idle men. It is in hand for now, and I would rather talk about you."

His indecision was fleeting, there would be plenty of time to talk about Birca. For now, he was happy to be the focus of Brenna's attention. Making their way to the back of the hall, they entered the new hallway that led to their bedchamber.

Pushing aside the curtain, he looked about. The room was much the same as he'd left it. The large bed, sitting raised on a small dais, was elaborately carved and covered in furs. The fire burned in a large hearth to the side, giving a warm glow to the room.

Brenna came to stand before him, her eyes darkened with desire. "Vali?" His name was soft on her lips.

Vali was sure it was not words that she wanted from him. He pulled her to him and wrapped one arm around her waist. His other hand snaked into her hair, his fingers digging beneath her immaculate braids.

Brenna's hands rested against his chest, but she did not resist. His mouth hovered above hers as he studied her eyes, seeing nothing but her own primal need. His hunger to taste and to touch was all-powerful, but Vali would not cross that line unless invited.

Her breathing was shallow, her breasts pressing against him. Her hands travelled down his chest, reaching the edge of his tunic. Releasing his grasp, he stepped back from her and tugged the tunic over his head. He hooked his thumbs in his trousers, and waited.

Brenna pulled the ties of her gown free, letting it fall to the ground. She closed the space between them, pushing Vali until the back of his legs reached the bed. He fell onto

the soft furs, his arms wrapping around Brenna as she straddled him.

Their mouths joined, hungry for each other. Teeth
clashed and tongues explored. Brenna leaned back, staring
down at him with eyes ablaze.

"Streð mik, Brenna." His cock was rock hard at the sight
of her. *His Valkyrie*.

Reaching for his hands, Brenna placed them on her
breasts. Vali rubbed his palms over her hardening buds,
taking a firmer grasp when she arched her back and ground
her sex along his length.

Pushing himself upright, he fisted his hand in her hair
and held her neck back, exposed to his lips. She moaned,
her eyes falling closed.

He feathered his tongue across her throat and down
towards her breast. His free hand plucked at her nipple
while his tongue found the other.

She moaned her encouragement. His tongue found the
other furled bud and sucked hard. She cried out, grinding
harder against him. He yearned to plunge himself inside
her, at the same time fearing the moment would come all
too soon.

Brenna pulled his mouth from her, pushing him roughly
onto the bed. "I need to taste you."

She wiggled down his thighs and onto the floor.
Kneeling between his legs, she pulled his trousers off,
allowing his manhood to spring free. Her hands ran along
his thighs until she cupped his balls. He gasped as they
tightened, aching at her touch.

"By the gods," he muttered as her tongue ran the length
of his shaft, licking the glistening tip. For a mere moment
of torment Brenna took the head of his cock into her hot,
wet mouth. He groaned and pulled her off him, knowing

he couldn't take another second without falling over the edge.

Grabbing her hips, he kept pulling her up until she straddled his face. Having been starved of this pleasure for months, he ran his tongue along her seam until he found her opening. His tongue plunged into her, his mouth taking as much of her as he could. He held her hips in place, not daring to give her an inch to move away from him as he sucked the sweet, musky essence from her.

Her moans grew louder as his tongue ploughed inside her. He moved one hand around until his fingers found her nub. She cried out as he caressed her, rubbing his fingers back and forth in time with his tongue.

"Vali!" His name echoed off the wooden beams as she found her release, her essence flowing into his mouth.

Pulling free, he pushed her back, using his knees to open her legs. He drove himself hard inside her, feeling her contract around his cock, her body still vibrating from his mouth. Animal instinct took over, he needed to possess her; take his fill while she screamed his name. His own voice rose in harmony with Brenna's as he thrust inside her hard and fast. Spots of colour danced before his eyes as he exploded deep within her.

Vali rolled to the side and collapsed onto the bed, bringing Brenna with him. His heart hammered like Thor himself was beating upon his anvil in his chest; his breathing was harsh and jagged. His hand gently stroked her back.

"I missed your body," he whispered.

"I could tell."

The chuckle was low in his throat. "Did you miss me?"

"Of course." She nestled in closer, her leg draping over his.

She looked at peace lying beside him. For a moment, he could believe they were back in Fornsigtuna, in the loft he slept in above the small workshop on his family's farm. He brushed his lips against hers, desire stirring again.

"Nei, Vali. You'll have to wait." Brenna pulled out of his reach and rose from the bed.

"Why must I wait?" he patted the bed." Come, I am not finished with you yet."

Her smile was wide as she bent down to retrieve her gown. "I must go." She slipped it over her head and tied the dress in place. "Ivar will be waiting for me."

"Ivar?" Since when had he taken on such a prominent role in governing Birca?

"Ja, we need to determine a punishment for the men who started the fight at the Ting." Brenna turned from him, focused on dressing.

"Gita, can you come and straighten my hair?" She called.

The curtain moved and Gita stepped inside, averting her eyes when she saw him lying naked on the bed.

Vali stomped across the bedchamber, his footfall muffled by the furs laid across the floor. He quickly gathered his clothing and dressed. He felt as though Brenna had taken what she needed, and was now discarding him. "Gita, arrange a feast for this evening. I wish to celebrate Lord Vali's return from his adventures."

Vali swallowed the bile that had risen in his throat. "My *adventures*?"

"Ja, I've yet to hear your stories and how the trade agreements were negotiated."

"As you wish," he said through gritted teeth. "We can discuss my *adventures* after you have finished your *work*."

Beneath his anger, Vali felt the sharp sting of hurt. It had been his choice to give up raiding and stay in Birca, and

Brenna's offer of trade envoy had suited both their needs. Or so he thought. The trip to the East had not been without danger. The negotiations had required patience and skill. Yet it felt like Brenna thought it had been an adventure for Vali while she'd been *working*.

3

*B*renna sighed. Vali was angry - she could see it in his tense stance, in the slight tick in his jaw. How quickly his homecoming had soured.

"Vali, I must attend to this situation." Brenna swallowed her growing frustration. She did not have time to placate him. "Please, tell me, did you make any of the trade agreements?"

He did not look away from her, but his eyes had grown cold. "Ja, all of the trade agreements we discussed have been put in place. The East are keen to trade with Birca."

Relief flooded her body; something had gone right. "That is pleasing."

Vali snorted, but held his tongue.

"What is it?" She wanted to move closer, to reach out and touch him, but knew if she did, she would be lost. And Ivar would come looking for her soon. She stood still, her heart aching as the distance between them expanded.

"I am glad I have pleased you, Jarl."

Brenna swore it was contempt she saw on his face. Why was he so angry?

"Vali, a lot has happened while you've been away," she tried to explain. "There is so much unrest and mistrust between the newcomers and the townspeople. A man bit another's ear off at the Ting."

"That must have been truly horrifying." His sarcasm dripped from every word. "To witness such a barbaric display."

Brenna hissed. Of all people, she thought Vali would be the one person she could rely on to understand... who she did not have to be Jarl for. It seemed he was as foolish as the men awaiting her to pass judgement.

"What is it you expected, Vali?" She crossed her arms in front of her, jaw clenching.

He was pulling his boots back on, sitting on the bed they'd shared only moments ago. "To not have you rush off to your work with another man as soon as you have what you wanted from me?"

She could not believe what she was hearing. "What? By the gods-"

His face was mottled with rage. "You said you wanted to rule beholden to no man, yet I find you consulting Ivar on matters that should be the decision of the Jarl alone."

"I am beholden to no man. Not Ivar! And not you! This is my bedchamber, in my hall, in my lands." Her body shook with barely contained fury.

"Ja, you are Jarl, Brenna. You made it clear you did not want me by your side. But you are more than happy for Ivar to stand with you?"

"You are not listening to me!"

"I don't need to listen when I can see."

She threw her hands up in the air. He was being ridiculous. "You see naught!"

A hostile energy permeated the room. For months she

had longed for Vali to join her once again in this chamber, but instead of light and love, dark clouds swirled with suspicion and anger.

Brenna held on to her temper for fear of it giving way to tears. She couldn't afford to break. Not now.

Inhaling a deep breath, she held her head high. She was Jarl.

"I can see you are busy." Vali's speech was tight as he drew himself up to his full height. "I will take my leave."

That wasn't what she wanted. Why was he being so difficult?

"Vali, please..."

He walked away, pausing at the curtain. He looked over his shoulder, his blue eyes as dark as a storm boring into her.

"Cut off his ear."

"What?"

"It is fair; take his ear," he repeated as he exited. The curtain falling behind him echoed in the silent bedchamber.

Brenna stamped her foot. Despite all that had passed between them, Vali could still be as infuriating now as when he was a boy. Nei, not just Vali. It felt as though all the men around her were incapable of behaving rationally. Except Ivar. At least he was trying to be useful. But Vali was right - she alone was the Jarl and she must settle this tension quickly.

She sighed, straightened her shoulders and called for a servant to bring the feuding men before her in the great hall.

· · ·

SHE RETURNED TO THE DAIS, finding Ivar waiting by her chair.

"Jarl, we have yet to determine how to proceed," Ivar muttered in her ear.

She held her hand up, her eyes warning Ivar to back off. He complied, with a small bow of his head. Standing before her chair, she glared at the men before her.

"Hjalmar Brynjarsson, you have no claim to Vragi Ulfertsson's land, nor his daughters. Any further breach of this decision will result in dire punishment."

Vragi sniffed, holding his head high as blood dripped from the side of his head.

"I will not tolerate fighting at the Ting - from anyone!"

The smirk which had begun to form on Hjalmar's face fell flat.

"We will learn to live together, to make Birca a great trading centre. Petty disagreements will not divide us." She glanced around the hall as she spoke, ensuring that her message went beyond the two men in front of her.

"Vragi Ulfertsson, your severed ear will remind you to speak with civility to our newest townsfolk."

A whisper of uncertainty sounded from those present.

"Hjalmar Brynjarsson, it is your actions that not only brought you before me, but extended your time in the Ting. We live in peace amongst ourselves in Birca and if you wish to remain here, you will do so peaceably. To remind you of the consequences of your actions, it is my decision that one of your ears will be cut from your head."

A cheer rose from the crowd.

"Let this be a lesson to all of you," she glowered at the faces staring back at her.

"Steinar." Brenna nodded at the guard closest to her.

She held up her hand to silence the crowd. She was far

from done. The guard restraining Hjalmar grasped his hair and pulled his head to the side. Steinar stepped forward, his knife in hand. With one swift cut, he held aloft the severed ear for all to see. Another cheer rose from the crowd.

With a wave of her hand, Brenna dismissed the Ting and turned towards her chambers. Weariness weighed down every bone in her body. This was not a part of ruling that she took any pleasure in.

Ivar followed her into the hallway. "Jarl, a word?"

She paused at the curtain. "Not now, Ivar."

The heavy linen closed behind her. Gita was waiting by the fire and Brenna was glad to throw off the mantle of ruler in her presence.

"Shall I draw you a bath, Jarl?" asked Gita.

Brenna gave the girl a grateful smile. Once named Jarl, Brenna had freed Gita from servitude, however she had chosen to remain in Brenna's service and had become her friend. "How many times must I tell you, call me Brenna."

Gita inclined her head. "Alright, but only when we are alone, Brenna."

They exchanged a smile.

"Now, about that bath?"

"Please, and a plate of food and some mead."

"Shall I see if the kitchen has any pig's ears?" Gita said, swallowing her smile.

The serving boy who had entered the chamber with a bucket of steaming water almost dropped it into the wooden bath.

Brenna burst out with laughter; Gita quickly followed suit. The boy scurried from the room, his face as hot as the flames in the fire pit. The tension in her shoulders began to lift and she was once again grateful for Gita and her friendship.

"Nei, I believe cheese and bread will be sufficient." She began removing the combs in her hair, then the amulet around her throat.

"Of course." Gita inclined her head and turned to leave the room. "A just sentence, if I may say so. How did you and Ivar think of it?"

The last of her laughter died on her lips. "Actually, it was Vali's suggestion."

"Vali is very clever, and occasionally wise." With a wink, she left for the kitchen.

Brenna looked around the bedchamber. Everything was in its place, yet the room felt so empty. As much as she was loathe to admit it, Vali - even in the midst of his anger, had offered the perfect solution to end the discord between the farmer and the warrior. She sat on the edge of the bed and began to unlace her boots.

Vali had returned; the man for which she had yearned for months, and yet she felt he was further away than before. She couldn't understand his sudden anger, nor his accusation that she was merely using him. He had seemed to enjoy their coupling as much as she did.

Pulling her feet out of her boots, she sighed. What had gotten into all the men in Birca today? They were all acting like fools.

4

_____

"Not that I haven't enjoyed your company, Vali, but do you think you'll be returning to your own lodgings soon?"

Although spoken gently, Nissa was sweeping the floor of the small house she and Frode were staying in while in Birca. Her deft stokes towards the door underlined her words as more of a suggestion than a question. Vali looked to Frode to find him staring pointedly back at him. It seemed in his efforts to avoid Brenna for the rest of the day, he'd overstayed his welcome in the tiny house. And in the process, put a hold on any plans Frode and Nissa had of getting reacquainted.

He sighed heavily. "I would if I had my own lodgings to return to."

"Thor's blood, you are stubborn. Your place is with Brenna!" Frode slammed his fist onto the table to make his point.

"Brenna is the Jarl and it is _her_ great hall. _Her_ chambers. She made that very clear." He rose from the table and took a step back. "What am I to the Jarl, other than her errand boy?"

"Oh Vali, you know that is not true," said Nissa, stilling the broom in her hands.

"Not that I can blame her for leaving you to sulk. You are behaving like an old goat!" added Frode.

"Agh," snapped Vali with a dismissive wave of his hand. He stood and headed for the door.

"We'll see you tonight at the feast," Frode called after him.

"It is true, we saw many strange and wonderful sights on our journey." Frode stood before an enraptured audience. "It seems people are more willing to share their secrets when we are there to trade, and not to plunder."

A wave of good-natured mockery echoed around the great hall. Vali stole a glance at Brenna. She was seated in the high chair next to him, leaning forward, her hands clasping the arm rests, so as not to miss a word of Frode's high-spirited account of their journey to the East.

"But I have saved the best thing until now," said Frode. "It is a gift from an important trader in Miklagaard."

Frode produced a small wooden box, removing the lid with a flourish.

"Inside is the bark of the cassia tree." He presented the box to Brenna. Inside lay three small, brown pieces of bark.

"The location of these cassia trees is a closely guarded secret," explained Vali. The room had fallen silent and his voice carried across the hall. "It has a distinctive scent."

Brenna looked from the box in her hand to Vali, before bending her head and inhaled, pulling back as the aroma filled her nostrils.

"It is spicy, but somehow also sweet," murmured Brenna.

She examined the contents of the box further. "Do you cook with it?"

"I believe the bark can be ground into a powder and it has many uses, including flavouring food," said Vali. "But the bark has a much more sacred use."

Vali took the box and handed it back to Frode.

"The bark of the cassia tree has long been an offering made only to those of importance." Frode held the box out so those seated closest to the fire pit could catch a glimpse of its contents. "The gods, ja. But also, kings and queens, emperors and emirs." He turned back to Brenna. "And Valkyries."

Vali heard her breath catch.

"It is said that when the cassia is cast into the fire, you are able to see the gods."

Muted exclamations and gasps erupted.

"Vali, have you seen this with your own eyes?" asked Brenna, her face shining in wonder and excitement.

"Nei," he replied. "This gift is for you."

They turned back to Frode, standing before the fire pit.

"With your permission, Jarl Brenna, we will crush one piece of the bark into powder in preparation for joining it with fire."

From the corner of his eye, Vali saw Brenna nod her assent.

Nissa stepped forward, a small bowl in her hands. Frode placed one piece of bark into the vessel. Nissa set to work crushing the cassia into a powder, all eyes in the great hall watching her movements. Moments later, she returned the bowl to him.

Standing before Brenna, Frode nodded then turned back to address the hall.

"Hail to Odin, Allfather and seeker of wisdom.

"Hail to Frigga whose gifts weave through our lives.

"Hail to Thor, strong-armed defender of Midgard.

"Hail to Sif, bringer of life to the cold earth.

"Hail to Frey, giver of wealth of gold and grain alike.

"Hail to Freya, who stirs sweet desire and keen-edged strife.

"Hail to Heimdall, the constant guardian of bright Bifrost,

"Hail to Njord, friend of sailors,

"Hail to Ran, both bane and reprieve of ships at sea.

"Hail to Balder, brightest son of farseeing Odin, final hope of the gods, final hope of all the worlds."

Digging his fingers into the bowl, Frode threw the powder across the fire pit. Flames immediately bent and curled, and the spicy aroma underlaid with sweetness filled the room.

Brenna and Vali stood as one. Vali could scarcely believe what was before his eyes. Figures emerged from the fire, riding upon winged stallions. Gods with powerful shoulders and knowing faces, goddesses with flowing hair and divine wisdom. Rising into the air for all to see.

"It truly is the gods," cried a voice from the crowd.

Vali had heard of the magic contained within this spice, but to stand witness to it was another matter altogether. He reached for Brenna's hand, curling his fingers around hers.

Abruptly, the flames seem to fold into each other - as though the gods no longer wished to remain on this earthly plane. The images dove back into the fire pit, leaving behind their lingering scent.

"Why did they return to the fire?" whispered Brenna.

"I do not know," said Vali. "Mayhap, that is the way of this magic."

"No," she replied. "It is as if they needed to escape."

A scream echoed in the distance.

Ivar was on his feet. "Did you hear that?"

Vali reached instinctively for his sword.

The doors of the great hall burst open, bringing the screams of the dead and dying from the outside in. "Jarl Brenna, we are under attack!"

Vali recognised the man as one of the town's oldest fishermen.

"Who dares to attack Birca?" bellowed Ivar.

The man shrank at the question, but stayed his ground. "It is your people."

Ivar frowned. "My people? You speak in riddles."

"The newcomers. They set their longhouse on fire and started slaughtering people. They say they fight in the name of King Gorm of Gyldarhagi."

"The *usurper* of Gyldarhagi!" hissed Brenna.

Warriors drew their weapons. Gita appeared at Brenna's side with her leather corset, shield and sword.

"We must identify the culprits," said Ivar, axe in hand.

Vali looked the man up and down with suspicion. "I believe they have already been identified."

"Did you know of this?" demanded Brenna of Ivar.

"Nei, Lady. I swear on my arm ring I knew naught. I cannot believe this is the work of all the newcomers."

We shall see, thought Vali.

"Defend the town and our people. Go!" growled Brenna.

Vali stepped forward, pausing as her hand caught his arm.

"I'm glad you're here," she said.

His heart warmed despite the adrenalin spiking through his veins. His earlier anger was forgotten as he inclined his head and placed his hands on her shoulders, looking into her eyes. "I will be here when you need me, always."

Brenna bit her lip and nodded. He ran his thumb over her cheek, watching as the fire went from a flicker to a flame in her eyes.

She reached up and squeezed his hand. "Let's fight."

5

*B*renna ran through the village with Vali and her warriors at her side; the smell of the longhouse burning and the anguished screams carried on the wind. The glow of the flames became a roaring inferno as they approached.

Brenna counted six men in a circle, widening by the second, as they swung their weapons upon the townspeople who ran forth to defend their home. At least a dozen bodies lay where they fell, all appeared to be farmers and traders. The reason was evident - the bloodlust in the eyes of the attackers burnt red and cruel. Brenna recognised each of these men as stragglers into Birca after the defeat of Sigurd. Clearly, they'd had a mission.

Her warriors roared their arrival into the fray, taking over the battle as the townspeople fell back and turned their attention to the burning building. The clash of sword and axe became more pronounced as Viking took on Viking.

Indignation burned through Brenna's veins. How dare these men take advantage of her readiness to forgive. How dare they slaughter innocents in her town.

She threw her shield to the ground, preferring an axe in one hand, her sword in the other. One of the attackers was gaining the upper hand over Ivar. Brenna let her fury lead her. Vengeance fuelled her war cry. Within three strides she was on the attacker, her axe slicing the back of his legs and her sword finding the opening in the side of his breastplate. A second swing of her axe finished him.

She roared in satisfaction.

Another of his comrades lunged for Brenna. She deflected his sword with her own, swiping the tops of his thighs, and no doubt his manhood with her axe. He howled louder than the battle, scrambling back to cover his wounds. Brenna swung the axe again, knocking him to the ground. Discarding his weapon, she grasped her sword with both hands, holding it in line with his throat. The blade sliced through skin and muscle before she felt the crack of bone separating as she reached the back of his neck.

We need one alive. Why would Gorm want to bring war on her?

She opened her mouth to give the order but was drowned out by the sound of the war horn coming from the docks. Someone was approaching!

Her warriors surrounded the last attacker still breathing, waiting for her command. Before she could speak, Ivar drove his sword through his chest. She pushed aside her frustration. The fight was not over yet.

Brenna looked around, finding a young boy standing with a farmer's axe in hand, wanting to fight. She beckoned him over.

"You wish to serve?" she asked, bending down to look him in the eye.

"Ja, Jarl Brenna. I want to fight with you." His eyes gleamed in the dulling firelight with childish anticipation.

"Nei, I have a much more important task for you."

He cocked his head to the side, disappointment jostling with curiosity.

"You must go to the great hall and find Gita. Do you know her?" The boy nodded. "We are under attack. I need my bravest warrior to ensure those that cannot fight get to safety in the mountains. You must find Gita and tell her to spread the word."

Brenna placed her hands on his shoulders. "And I need you to lead the people of Birca to safety. Can you do that for me?"

"Ja, Jarl." His eyes glowed with pride. "I can do this."

"Good," she nodded once. "May the gods go with you."

The boy ran towards the market place, bound for the hall. Brenna rose to her feet as another warrior appeared.

"Frode?"

"Ja, it is I."

"Nissa is safe?"

"She will head for the mountains."

"Can you gather more men and bring them to the docks, take two more of the men. I fear a bigger attack is almost upon us."

Frode wasted no time, heading for the longhouses.

"Ivar," she turned to face him, "why did no other warriors appear to help defend the town and stop these men?"

He wiped blood that did not belong to him from his face. "By the gods, I wish I knew."

"Is it possible that all of the newcomers are against us?" Vali gave voice to the question circling her own mind.

Ivar shook his head. "Nei, I cannot believe it."

Frustration boiled in her veins. "Yet so many have

warned me that this may be the case. And now I find they are not here to fight when they are needed."

"I beg your pardon, Jarl, but neither were Birca's own warriors."

Her veins turned to ice. What was this treachery? Had all her warriors deserted her? Was her rule so poorly supported? A scream raged between her ears, trapped inside.

The battle horn sounded again.

"We must get to the docks." She forced her legs to carry her forward, bending to retrieve her axe after sheathing her sword. Vali handed her the shield she'd discarded as they made for the water.

With relief she saw at least three dozen men waiting on the banks of the fjord, along with her look outs. Sliding through the dark waters, the shape of three drakkars appeared.

"Can you make out the flag?" asked Vali.

"Nei," came the muttered responses.

"The attackers said they were acting on behalf of Gorm of Gyldarhagi," said another.

"If that is the case, the flags will bear a raven in flight with eyes as red as Hel's own fire," said Ivar.

Brenna tightened her grip on the handle of her axe. She could see no reason for Gorm to attack her land, but she would relish the opportunity to take his head from his shoulders and return the throne to her mother's family.

"We need to make ready." She looked about; no other warriors had joined them. "Where is Frode and my army?"

As the words left her lips, heavy footfall sounded behind her. Finally! Frode made his way to her side.

"Jarl Brenna, your warriors were locked inside their

longhouses." His eyes were wide, as though not quite believing what he was saying.

"All of them?"

"Ja, they tried to get out when they heard the fighting and smelt the smoke, but the doors were barred from the outside. They are on their way here now."

Relief and fury danced together inside.

"I think they planned to set them all on fire once they had blocked any chance of escape."

Fear punched her hard in the belly. "The longhouse that burned?"

"Was full."

"Did anyone escape?"

Frode shook his head.

Stereo mik! The traitors had left only the elderly and the young with any chance of defending the town.

"And those in the great hall?" Her voice rasped with fear.

"They live. It would seem they wanted to give Gorm someone to kill when he arrived." Frode jerked his head toward the approaching boats.

Gorm stood at the bow of the boat, illuminated by torch light; the usurper of her mother's family's throne. The very sight of him disgusted her. Dirty blonde hair was held back from his face with a thick, golden circlet fixed upon his head. Tattoos on his face and neck joined with those across his torso. Aside from gold arm bracers, he wore no other armour. Dark trousers covered thick thighs. He held his weapons, a double-headed axe and his sword, by his side. Evil washed off him in waves, carrying him and his army closer to shore.

Brenna swallowed her anguish. There would be time to grieve the dead after the impending battle. Her army was gathering behind her, confused and angry. This would not do. Now she would see if the newcomers could fight with her warriors as one. She called for her hersirs. They needed a plan, and fast.

6

*T*he moon reflected off the fjord, casting an eerie pall as Vali wiped the blood of his enemy from his face and surveyed the battle.

Metal clashed with metal.

Blood lust harmonised with death cries.

Odin's Valkyries would be kept busy on this night.

Gorm and his men had swarmed the beach, unable to penetrate Birca's shield wall in their early attempts. Outrage fused the newcomers with the town's warriors, all united by a refusal to bow to the warmonger's demands.

Vali caught glimpses of Gorm from afar. As big as his warriors were, the false king seemed to stand taller and broader than anyone else. He hoped the gods saw fit to cross his path with the usurper before the battle was won.

Pure energy coursed through his veins, as familiar as it was welcome. Vali may have turned his back on raiding, but he was Viking and battle was his lifeblood. The scuffle at the longhouse had reignited a flame that now burned with a beautiful fury as he wielded his axe and sword against enemy combatants. He had abandoned his shield long ago, enabling him to pivot and thrust with each new partner as the previous one fell in his dance of death.

He stretched his neck from side to side.

It is not your time, my son.

As he inclined his head towards the words, the lightning strike of a spear grazed his ear. He felt the strength of his ancestors at his side; the spirit of his father joining him as he roared at another failed attempt to dispatch him to Valhalla.

The invading army was strong, and disciplined. Mayhap they expected a weaker quarry? But they fought on, preferring death to retreat. Little by little, they forced the people of Birca back from the beach.

Frustration boiled in Vali. Dawn was still hours away and the dark provided a protective veil around the invaders until they materialised from the sea to replace those that were felled. He felt his face and body slick with the blood of other men. He felt the swell of Birca's warriors retreat to higher ground. Still, he fought on.

"Fall back!" came the cry.

Vali bellowed his disagreement with the order, and swung his axe to meet another's sword. He plunged his own into an unprotected thigh, spinning to give his axe enough power to take the head from its shoulders. They kept coming. Vali greeted them with a malevolent grin.

BRENNA FELT the heaviness of her sword and axe extend into her arms, slowing her thrusts, fatigue beginning to assert itself. Her sword reverberated off the axe of a man twice her size. She gritted her teeth and swung her own axe at his shins.

He stood his ground, but his guttural roar let her know she had split skin.

Using the momentum to swing her around, her sword connected with his arm.

Still, the man-mountain did not fall.

She dragged some oxygen into her lungs, knowing he was wearing her down. Arching backwards to avoid his thrust, she allowed herself to keep moving away from him.

He took the opportunity to straighten, find his footing.

Brenna launched herself at him, aiming for his injured arm. Her sword found its target and at last he toppled to his knees. She continued her swing until her axe sliced into his neck. Her boot found his face, freeing her axe and forcing him into the mud. Her visceral scream rolled across his lifeless form.

With weapons at the ready, she surveyed the battlefield. Too many were dead and dying. Her army grew weaker while her enemy was relentless.

Unlike Sigurd, Gorm did not watch the fight from afar. He fought harder and bloodier than any other warrior. His desire for victory or death was clear. With a flick of his wrist, he drove his sword into the face of one of her men.

As if sensing her, his eyes collided with hers.

The clatter of battle faded, while it continued to rage around them both.

"You, Brenna Ragnarsdotter, will fulfil the destiny of your ancestors," came the voice of the Seer, echoing from her past. *"You will heal the scars that run deep in their veins."*

"The gods are all around," she whispered. It was time to seek vengeance for her ancestors.

Brenna moved toward him, allowing fate to guide her feet. She saw one of her men launch himself at Gorm. He kept his eyes trained on her alone, thrusting his sword into the gut of her warrior.

Still, she continued forward.

Gorm opened his mouth. She heard him laugh. Was he mocking her?

"Enough!"

His order thundered over the beach and across Birca. The battle paused and the dark held its silence.

"I would speak with you, Jarl Brenna," he enunciated every syllable, her name grinding into dust as it left his mouth. "And offer you a chance to stop the slaughter of your people."

Brenna noted how his chest rose and fell evenly, as though the fight had not even brokered a sweat from him. A gash across his bare chest intermingled his own blood with the blood of those he'd slain. She looked into his eyes and saw the flames of Hel reflected in their void. The terror of those damned to the underworld reached out and scratched their fingers over her flesh.

She held his stare. "You wish to negotiate?"

"I do," he closed the ground between them. "Jarl and shield maiden." He breathed the words against her ear like a caress.

Her warriors closed in around them, their weapons raised. She held her hand up, letting them know to stand down. All the same, her fingers gripped the hilt of her sword even though he was too close for her to raise it against him.

"What do you want?" She refused to speak his name.

Gorm completed a slow circle around her. She raised her chin as he looked her up and down. A frown settled on his brow and something unknown passed across his face.

"Daughter of Ragnar, who is your mother?"

Shock quickly gave way to anger. How dare this man speak of her mother.

"My mother is Hertha, cousin to Ingrid of Gyldarhargi," she hissed. "The rightful heir to the throne you stole."

Gorm seemed not to notice the venom in her tone as he considered her words, the corners of his mouth lifting into a mirthless smile. "That is even better," he murmured.

Confusion warred with her anger. What did that matter to the Usurper? Despite the myriad of questions begging to be asked, Brenna held her tongue.

"What I want is to offer you the opportunity to return your family to the throne of Gyldarhagi."

All the air escaped from her lungs. "You wish to renounce your claim?"

His laugh was as harsh to her ears as one hundred cuts from a knife across her face. Her mind raced to understand. What game was Gorm playing with her? Clearly, he wanted Birca. Then he would own the lands on either side of King Aric's stronghold.

"I'll not relinquish Birca; not even for my mother's birthright."

His laugh had become a low rumble. "Little Jarl…"

Indignation bristled up her spine.

"You will not have to relinquish Birca. What I'm proposing is that you rule both Birca and Gyldarhagi, by my side." He leaned in until his face was close enough for her to see the blood and mud encrusted in the wrinkles around his eyes. "As my wife."

Disgust roiled in her belly. Of course. After everything she'd been through to become the Jarl of Birca, she still remained a pawn for men and territory. If she'd not left her dagger buried in the gut of an attacker, she would use it against Gorm this instant.

Gorm pulled back, silently watching her.

The battle that raged inside would be evident to him as they stood face to face. No, she would not give him that. Not even a hint of the trepidation that raged within. What she needed was time. Time for Aric to raise his army and come to her aid.

"That is a lot to consider, Lord Gorm." She swallowed the bitter taste of the niceties she'd forced from her mouth. "Would you give me the day to consider?"

"What is there to consider? To stop the bloodlust, I am offering you the chance to double your territory and rule with me."

"I must speak with my council."

He raised his axe in the air. "I think I understand. You wish to say your goodbyes to your lover, ja?"

Every nerve ending clenched as she struggled to control the outburst that threatened to erupt. The impudence of the brute!

"But do not think to marry him, Jarl Brenna."

She narrowed her gaze.

"Marriage to another would only result in his death." A cruel smile split his scarred face. "In much the same way my son dispatched your previous husband."

Dreaded comprehension formed. *Sigurd was the son of Gorm?*

7

"So, Sigurd the Black was the bastard son of Gorm," said Vali, pacing the length of the oblong fire pit in the centre of the great hall.

"And Gorm is here to avenge his death?" asked Torsten, one of Brenna's council men.

"While he did not say that precisely, it seems the logical conclusion," agreed Brenna.

Brenna, Vali, Eric, Snorri and Ivar still wore their battle clothes; covered in blood and mud. In stark contrast, the four members of the council wore pristine tunics and furs, and sat well back from the warriors on a separate table.

"At least he agreed that both sides could remove their dead and tend to their wounded during the parley," she said.

Gorm and his army had set up camp on the banks of the fjord, further along from the battlefield. Plumes of smoke from the burial pyres had welcomed the rising sun on the blood-kissed beach.

Vali slammed his hand against the table. "He does you no favours, Brenna. The callous laughter of his men as they eat and bathe only fuels the bitterness festering amongst Birca."

She gave him a tired look but did not argue. Instead, Brenna motioned for the servants to bring food and ale. He swallowed his frustration at the sight of her, covered in blood, almost slouching in her chair from exhaustion.

"It seems that father and son are alike, Jarl Brenna," said Torsten. "Gorm has determined that you will be his ultimate prize."

"Nei," she sighed. "I believe I am merely a pawn in the game."

Vali could feel the depths of Brenna's dispirit. She'd sworn to never again find herself in this position. He turned his attention to the fire pit. Was it only hours ago he'd watched the gods rise from these very flames, only to return as the fighting erupted?

"A pawn," asked Torsten.

"To what end?" asked another council member.

"If Gorm rules over Gyldarhagi and Birca, he effectively surrounds Fornsigtuna and the rest of King Aric's territories. He would be able to launch attacks from both sides," said Brenna.

"And become King of all of Svealand." Vali spoke to the depths of the fire. He could see the insult of Gorm's proposal. He could see it all.

"Surely not," said Torsten. "Not even Aric has moved against Gyldarghagi to claim such a title."

"Who would take on Gorm? 'Tis a gift from the gods that he has left these lands alone until now," said another.

"And even the gods fled when Gorm attacked," said Ivar, whose appetite appeared not to have suffered. He called for more ale to wash the last of his meat and bread down.

Vali bristled at his words. The man set his teeth on edge,

and he was sure it was not just because of his closeness with Brenna. There was something treacherous about Ivar - he could feel it in his bones.

"You stood firm, Ivar. As if you had nothing to fear in the battle ahead." Vali turned from the fire to face him.

"What should I fear? The defeat of my enemy, or Valhalla?" Ivar mopped the grease from his trencher with his bread.

"Ivar, let me ask you this. In this battle, which side is your enemy?"

A heady tension enveloped the room. Vali noticed Brenna sit up straighter in her chair.

Ivar chuckled. "What sort of question is that?" He drained the ale from his drinking horn.

"An important one, I think."

"Vali? What are you saying?" asked Brenna, the blood and mud of battle still stained her face and armour.

He rose from his seat, sliding his gaze around those in the hall. "Frode told us that all of our warriors were locked inside their lodgings. Yet the night was young. How is it possible that every warrior and shield maiden had taken to their bed so early?"

Uncertainty ricocheted amongst the council. All had stilled, waiting for the answer.

"There is a simple answer, Vali," said Ivar. "You know of the trouble between the newcomers and the townspeople since Jarl Brenna defeated Sigurd the Black." He shrugged. "I had planned to take all the warriors on a training camp in order for them to come together as one army. We were to leave before dawn."

"That seems rather convenient." Vali's gut continued to churn with doubt.

"Nei." Ivar looked at him. "What would have been

convenient is if none of Brenna's warriors were in the town when Gorm attacked."

A collective exhalation diffused the tension in the hall.

"Enough of this." Brenna rose from her chair. "The traitors in this town revealed themselves and met their fate. We must focus on the enemy camped on our shores, not look for them here."

Her stare came to rest on Vali.

He could not shake his suspicions about Ivar, but he would put them aside until he could speak with Brenna alone. He nodded his assent.

"What do you propose, Jarl?" asked Torsten.

"We have until the end of the day to decide," she began. "And we shall take every moment available to us."

"We lost a lot of men," said Ivar.

Brenna nodded. "Ja, but so did Gorm. I will send a scout to determine their numbers."

"And I will go to our warriors and see what is left of our army," said Eric. "Hopefully King Aric is on his way."

"And if he's not?" asked Torsten. "Will you consider Gorm's offer, Jarl?"

Vali stiffened. "She will not!" He slammed both hands on the table across from Torsten.

"We must consider our people. If fighting means annihilation-" the councillor started.

"Nei, the gods would not allow Brenna to lose her land and her title," hissed Vali.

Torsten rose and stepped forward. "If she married Gorm, she would lose neither."

"And our people would survive," said Brenna, her voice barely audible.

Vali spun to face Brenna. "You would not consider this?"

"I am Jarl. I must consider everything."

He looked at each of the men gathered in the great hall. Most avoided his gaze. The blood boiled in his veins. He moved toward Brenna. If the decision was left to these rass-ragr, they would marry her off to save themselves.

He paused in front of her, his eyes pleading with her. "What of the prophecy?"

"What is a prophecy if not the dreams of another," said Ivar. "And I have never put much stead in dreams."

He clenched his fists and set his jaw. "You would question the gods?"

"Nei, Vali. I would question those that say they speak for the gods. "

Ivar stood, the blood and sweat of battle ingrained on his face and armour. "The prophecy never made mention of you, Vali. Mayhap the gods have another fate planned for you. Besides, if the Jarl marries Gorm, the prophecy remains true. Does it not?"

Vali locked eyes with Brenna, finding confusion in their depths. She looked away.

An icy chill coiled around his heart as he watched Ivar swagger toward the door. Damn that níðingr, for his words rang with some truth.

8

*B*renna sat on a stool in front of the fire in her bedchamber. In the name of Frigga, she needed to clear her mind of men and their arguments. Her lands were under threat and she must make a decision. But what of her choices? Even if she married Gorm, this was no guarantee of her people's safety. But to fight without Aric would lead to devastating losses? She was weary of watching her people die. Her mind ran round and round, seeing no clear answer.

The heavy fabric separating her private chambers from the main hall moved aside; Vali had followed her.

"They've set a guard outside and in the great hall," he said.

She nodded. There was no reason to trust Gorm would keep his word and wait until the end of the day for her response to his terms.

A bath steamed next to the fire and her aching body longed to feel its healing warmth. Her fingers worked the laces holding her arms bracers in place.

On orders from Brenna, only a few of the servants had

returned from their hiding place in the mountains, including Gita.

"Jarl, let me help you," the young woman said, appearing from the side chamber.

"That won't be necessary, Gita," said Vali. "I will assist the Jarl."

Gita looked to Brenna for her agreement, and then withdrew.

Vali walked to the pitcher of mead that sat on a side table, poured a tankard and brought it to her.

Taking it from him, she looked up into his face, as battle weary as her own. Naught knew her better than Vali. And now, for one moment, she wanted to forget she was Jarl, carrying the weight of the future and wellbeing of her people. She needed to just be Brenna, alone with the boy she'd always loved.

Brenna extended her arm, allowing Vali to finish unlacing the leather fastenings.

"Are you wounded?" he murmured.

"Nei." She took a sip of the mead. "Are you well?"

He nodded, the corner of his mouth lifting into a smile as he slipped off the first bracer. She moved the tankard to her other hand.

"I am tired," she said.

"Will you sleep?"

"Nei."

He removed the second bracer and started on her leather corset.

"I'd forgotten what it felt like, to fight," he said. "To feel the sword in my hand, the swing of the axe."

"You missed it?"

He took the tankard from her hand, placing it on the

table. Gently, he pulled the corset free. "I would not say I missed it. I relished the battle once it was upon me."

"You fought well."

"As did you, shield maiden."

She bowed her head to hide the smile his words evoked. Raising her arms above her, she felt the weight of the mail she wore lift in his hands. Once becoming Jarl, her council had insisted she wear this extra layer of protection. She'd trained for many weeks to become used to the heavy shirt under her corset. Now, she barely noticed it until it was removed.

Finally, she stood in her trousers and tunic. Sinking onto a bench, she set about removing her boots while Vali saw to his own coverings.

Gita returned momentarily, to take their discarded armour for cleaning.

"Come," Vali held his hand out to her.

She let him pull her to her feet, coming to stand toe to toe with him. He tucked a lock of hair that had come loose from her braid behind her ear, the palm of his hand cradling her cheek. His tender touch soothed her mind and slowed her thoughts.

Reaching for the bottom of her tunic, he lifted it over her head, his fingers sending a shiver over her skin as they trailed over her hips and ribs, then along her arms. Her nipples stood at attention in the cool air, alert to his touch as her trousers slipped to the floor.

He led her to the bath, guiding her into its welcoming depths. Her body immediately felt lighter, the tension of battle and politics receding in her limbs. Vali gently began to untangle the braids from her hair. No words were exchanged while he washed the blood and sweat from her hair and body. His firm hands on her body and scalp made her feel safe, taking her mind from her troubles.

Once she was clean, he removed his clothes and joined her, facing her in the water. The tub was large, designed for a Jarl. But the water sloshed over the edge and legs entangled to accommodate both bodies.

"Your ribs are bruised," she observed.

"But not cracked," he said.

She watched him scrub the grime from his body, admiring the way his muscles glistened with the combination of firelight and water. He sponged the blood and mud from his long braid. The sides of his head were freshly shaved, revealing the intricate tattoo of a warrior wolf inked into his skull.

Water cascaded down her body as she rose, stepping out of the tub. She wrapped herself in linen before fetching a clean jug of water, pouring it over Vali's head and shoulders to rid the last remnants of the battle from his body.

He accepted the linen she held out for him, their fingers touching as the cloth was exchanged. As he rubbed himself dry in front of the fire, Brenna soaked in the sight of his body, tall and muscled. His shoulders were broad and his legs strong. Desire stirred within.

Dropping the linen to the floor, she crawled onto the bed.

"Vali." Her tone was heavy with need.

His eyes roamed her body, his eyes darkening while his cock stirred with lust.

She parted her legs, encouraging him to join her. Her body ached for his touch.

He poured himself some mead, his eyes never leaving hers. Her heartbeat quickened under his gaze, her hunger growing by the second. He drained his tankard and finally came to bed, moving his body over hers.

His lips brushed against her lips, his weight above her igniting the flame inside. Arching against him, she surrendered to the sensation, knowing it was the one thing that could release her from her burdens, if only for a short time.

Soft kisses feathered her face, her throat, finding her breasts. His hands were soft, offering a reprieve from the heavy strikes of battle. She resisted the urge to hasten the slowly-building pleasure and push his face upon her womanhood. She gave over all control to Vali, allowing him to lead her to the edge.

He continued across her stomach, his mouth exploring the angle of her hips before his tongue began tracing patterns down her thighs. She twisted her hands in the furs she lay on; the torture exquisite. An eternity passed before he pressed his lips against her slick folds; soft moans underscoring his gentle lapping.

Lightning bolts of ecstasy accompanied the probing of his tongue. She opened her legs wider, urging the wave to crest inside her.

Vali kept his steady rhythm, even as she whimpered for more.

"More, please..."

He held her firm, his hand pressed against her stomach to prevent escape.

By the gods, he knew just how to please her. She grasped the furs tighter. Finally, the swell took form, rushing to its peak. She cried out to the gods as the waves crashed all around her.

Her body was still shuddering as Vali slipped his length inside her, filling her senses and reigniting her orgasm. He lifted her hips and hooked her legs around him. His eyes locked on hers, and she couldn't look away. His cock thrust faster than his tongue had and she was lost to everything, except him. Pleasure consumed her, their cries combining as he filled her with his seed.

They collapsed onto the bed, Brenna still quivering from their passion.

Vali pressed his lips against her forehead. "I love you, Brenna."

Her mouth curled into a smile. It seemed the goddess had heard her plea.

9

The gods granted Vali and Brenna three hours of rest before they were roused. Their battle dress lay clean and waiting, although there was no sign of Gita.

Vali pulled his leather jerkin into place.

Brenna moved in to take the straps from him. "Let me help you."

"My thanks." He raised his left arm for her to tie the fastenings.

A heavy stone sat in the pit of his stomach. But of all the concerns filling his mind, his distrust of Ivar was the most pressing. He knew Brenna trusted the man and had relied on him to ease the transition of the newcomers from Sigurd's army, but he could no longer hold his tongue. He had only moments before they would need to continue discussions with the council.

"In the weeks before I left for the East," he began. "While I wouldn't say the people were at ease with the newcomers from Sigurd's army, they trusted in your decision to bring these men in to bolster our defences and keep the town safe."

Brenna raised her eyes to his. "Turn, please?"

He turned so she could reach the other side opening, then continued on.

"Since my return, the unease has flourished into outright tension, and even hatred. It seems Ivar is no longer able to command his men."

"Ivar is not in command of those men - Eric and Snorri are my hersirs." Her voice was light but Vali knew her well enough to hear the annoyance beneath her words.

"So, what is Ivar's role here?"

"He knows these men. He acts as an emissary, of sorts." Brenna gave the knot a hard tug. "And I believe it is important for the men to see one of them holding an important role in my council."

Sordinn! Vali did not have a place on her council.

"Ivar is a member of council?"

She hesitated. "Not officially." She gave him a hard look. "What evidence do you have that Ivar is not loyal to me?"

Vali frowned. "It is only a feeling," he admitted. It was not his intention to anger her, only to convince her to consider another point of view.

"Well then, can we focus on what is real?"

Rather than risk an argument, he changed the topic. "Do you believe we will learn more today about the uprising from within Birca?"

Sighing, she tugged the final strap into place. "It is hard to say. It seems the truth to their betrayal may have died with them. I know naught of any of my other warriors turning to fight with Gorm, suggesting they were not part of the plan."

She picked up his leather arm bracers and held them out for him to put in place. "Gita said the only talk of it from those taking shelter in the mountains was of disbelief. Who else might I speak with?"

"The men had no family here, no women folk or friends still breathing?"

Brenna closed the knot on the last of his bracer. "Torsten was looking into this. We shall see what he has to say."

Vali took her shirt of mail and held it out for her to slip over her head and onto her body. A question was on the tip of his tongue, but he did not want to sound belligerent.

"And who is speaking with Ivar?" he asked lightly.

She stilled her hands holding her leather corset, a hint of ice in her blue eyes. "What would be the purpose of speaking with Ivar on this matter?"

"He knew these men."

"Ja, that's true." She pulled the corset into place, allowing Vali to attend to the fastenings.

He kept his voice soft, not wishing to argue with her. "Mayhap, he could speak to their characters... and their loyalties."

He felt her tense. "Surely, if he thought their loyalties lay outside of Birca, Ivar would have brought this information to me."

"Unless," he paused to look her in the eye. "He had reason not to."

Brenna tilted her head. "Why do you believe Ivar to be a traitor to me?"

"He was very quick to pledge his loyalty to you at Tingvalla."

"I had just killed his master - Ivar had no warning of that. How would he have had time to form an alliance with Gorm?"

Vali shrugged. "Mayhap the alliance was already in place?"

"While that may be true, how could Ivar have known that Sigurd would be defeated that day?"

He struggled to keep his frustration at bay. "Don't you see? Look at the questions we have raised just now. There is much we do not actually know when it comes to Ivar and his relationship with Gorm."

Brenna shook her head. "I cannot believe it. Vali, you were gone for many months. You did not see how loyal Ivar has been."

Mayhap she was too close to the situation to see what he saw? He placed his hands on her shoulders, waiting for her eyes to meet his. "It is a feeling I cannot shake. I do not trust Ivar."

"But I do."

He studied her face, as he searched his heart. It was not jealousy of Ivar that motivated him to speak. This feeling in his gut was born of experience and instinct. Ivar could not be trusted. It seemed it would be up to him, alone, to watch the man. And he would do that. For Brenna and for Birca.

"And what of your decision today?" he asked.

She bowed her head until it rested on his chest.

Vali breathed in the scent of her hair, muted notes of smoke and sweat underlay her natural, sweet bouquet. He resisted the need to hold her tighter, to never let her go.

"I cannot marry that monster," she whispered.

Relief eased some of the tension across his shoulders.

"But without Aric, I fear we cannot hold Gorm off."

"Aric may arrive at any moment."

She pulled back. "I must convince the council to fight; to make a plan that will help us prevail."

"We will convince them, together."

Vali may not have changed her mind about Ivar, but at least he knew he had her heart.

BRENNA AND VALI joined her council as they reconvened in the great hall. Without word from Aric, the mood was tense. Servants had brought platters of cold meats, bread and cheese, as well as pitchers of ale. There was little discussion as they filled their bellies.

"Have the warriors been fed?" Brenna asked Gita.

"Ja, Jarl."

Brenna nodded and joined the men. "Torsten, did you learn anymore about the uprising?"

Torsten reached for his tankard and took a long swallow. "Jarl, it seems these men were acting alone."

"Friends, whores?" asked Ivar.

"Nei."

"These men came with you, Ivar," said Vali, eyeing the man across the table. "What do you know of them?"

Ivar raised his shoulders. "Not much. But if memory serves, they arrived a day or so after Jarl Brenna and the rest of us returned."

"Time enough to make a pact against Brenna," said Vali.

"Or to reconsider where their next meal was coming from," retorted Ivar.

"I believe we have more pressing matters to discuss," interrupted Brenna. She watched as Vali took a deep breath, his fists clenched. She shook her head and bit into the roast chicken on her trencher.

"Agreed," said Torsten. The older man stood. He was once a warrior of little renown, lean and reddish hair thinning to grey. He was known to have a good mind for the law, and Jarl Beinersson had relied on him for support in matters brought before the Ting.

Lately, however, Ivar had been a more vocal adviser than

Torsten. In fact, the council had allowed Ivar to speak on their behalf more often than not. Was it their fear of her, as Gita had suggested, or their trust in Ivar that quietened their tongues?

"We have had no word from King Aric and we do not know if he will support us against Gorm," began Torsten.

"I do not believe the King would allow Birca to fall into the hands of his enemy," said Brenna.

Torsten inclined his head. "True, Jarl. However, we must consider that even if Aric will support us, he may not reach us in time." He turned, gesturing to all present. "We must consider what is in the best interest of Birca."

And the best interest of the council, she thought.

"What of our army, Eric?" asked Vali.

"We have lost about thirty warriors, with another twenty or so too wounded to hold an axe."

Brenna dug her nails into the palm of her hands, silently cursing Gorm for bringing death to her land.

"And Gorm's men?"

Eric shook his head. "It is hard to tell. Mayhap they have lost as many, but it seems they were double our numbers before the battle began."

She scowled. His proposal of marriage needn't have involved bloodshed; Gorm and his men had engaged in battle for the sport of it.

"Without King Aric and his army, we cannot defeat Gorm," said Torsten.

Brenna looked to each of her advisers. Of course, Torsten would have spoken with the council and determined how they would each vote prior to this meeting. She doubted Ivar or her hersirs had been consulted, and certainly Vali had not. That meant four men would vote to end the bloodshed with an alliance of marriage. She felt

Ivar, Eric and Snorri would side with her and Vali. As Jarl, she could order them to fight. But she would prefer the council support her decision to fight for Birca in order to ensure everyone in the town would stand united with her.

"Our enemy may have had far greater numbers, but the gods were with us in battle." She stood and began to move around the hall. "We held Gorm and his army on the beach. They did not breach the town and they did not defeat us."

"But Jarl, with all respect to you and the gods," said Torsten. "Our warriors were losing ground."

"Yet it was Gorm who called for the fighting to halt," retorted Brenna, spinning around to face him.

"He knew he had gained the upper hand, Jarl-"

"Are you suggesting Birca would have fallen, Torsten?" The man hadn't even been on the battlefield!

"Jarl Brenna, I am suggesting our warriors were beginning to tire and were outnumbered. It was the right time for Gorm to set out his terms."

The blood began to simmer in her veins. Partly, because she did not want an alliance of marriage with the monster who had murdered her mother's family, and partly because she would have done the same thing as Gorm at that stage of the battle.

"So, we should just...give in to his demands?"

Torsten took a deep breath. "I believe we should give serious thought to Gorm's proposal of an alliance in order to avoid further death and bloodshed for our people."

She straightened her shoulders. It was difficult to argue with men who preferred to sit and talk about the gods rather than honour them on the battlefield.

From across the room, Brenna saw Vali uncross his arms and sit up straighter on the bench.

"Have you thought what this alliance would mean for you, Torsten? And the rest of the council?" Vali said softly.

Brenna felt a fissure of concern spark around the room. All eyes turned to Vali.

He continued, leaning back from the table. "What need would Gorm have of this council?"

"But we will agree to his terms," said another.

A smirk drifted across Vali's face. "So what?"

"If we agree to terms-"

"It will mean nothing to Gorm. Why would he keep a council that he has not chosen? A council that may be tempted to conspire against him?"

"It's true," said Brenna, marvelling at how brilliantly Vali had turned the room unanimously in her favour. "I would not keep the council in place."

She nodded her thanks to Vali as the council members exchanged looks of horror.

"Ivar, you have not shared your thoughts," said Vali.

Brenna heard a challenge underlying his tone. Was he really going to bring this up again? This animosity between the two men was becoming a problem.

"What can I say, Vali? You are right. Of course, Gorm will kill anyone he feels may stand in his way."

"It seems there is no way to avoid bloodshed," said Vali.

"So, we fight?" asked a council member.

"Victory or Valhalla," said Vali.

Ivar raised his drinking horn. "Skal."

Brenna nodded in satisfaction. She and Vali had achieved what they set out to do, yet his mistrust of Ivar grated. How little Vali must think of her instincts. She shook the thought from her mind and went out in search of a practical distraction.

10

*T*he town was devoid of its usual babble, replaced with the sounds of preparation for war. Even the wind held its breath, not stirring the falling autumn leaves, instead waiting to see what would happen when the battle began once more.

Brenna had dispatched scouts to ensure Gorm had no reserves waiting beyond the mountains to join the fight. The enemy may outnumber them, but they were camped on her beach. She met with her hersirs in the hall to determine their plan.

"Eric and I will each take a small group of archers to higher ground on either side of the beach in order to agitate Gorm's forces," said Snorri.

"Excellent," said Brenna. "I will lead our main army to meet Gorm on the beach."

They discussed the finer details, then Eric and Snorri left to inform their warriors and shield maidens of the plan.

Brenna went in search of the gothi, Hervor, to make a sacrifice to the gods to ask for strength and luck in the coming battle. Gita and the remaining servants set about boiling the meat for the warriors to eat before the fighting commenced.

"Is there no word from King Aric?" asked Vali, coming to stand beside her as she watched her army make their final preparations in the training yard.

"Nei." She released a heavy sigh.

"It would take some time to bring his army together and march to Birca." Vali gave her arm a gentle squeeze.

"I agree. I was hoping to have word from a messenger at least," she said. She found a smile for Vali, grateful he did not broach the subject of Ivar again. "I must go and speak with my warriors."

Her people had not been idle in the daylight hours; readying their arms and reinforcing the battlements that had been hastily set in place the previous evening. The wounded had already been moved to the great hall in readiness for the fight. Regardless of who the gods saw fit to bring victory to, the great hall would be the least likely building to be destroyed. Brenna ordered the remaining servants and townspeople to return to the mountains.

"Gita, why are you still here?" asked Brenna when Gita appeared at the training yard in battle dress, a borrowed shield on her arm and sword sheathed at her side.

"I am not needed in the mountains," she replied. "I can fight."

Brenna swallowed the words born of fear that sat at the tip of her tongue. "Gita, your strength and loyalty means everything to me."

"Then let me fight for you."

She smiled at her friend. Gita was tough and loyal. But she was not a shield maiden. Brenna could not risk losing her on the battlefield. "This army - Gorm's men - they are fierce and relentless. They will show you no mercy."

The shield sat awkwardly on Gita's arm, her sword catching against her dress.

"In which case the Valkyrie's may see fit to take me to Valhalla." Her words sounded even braver against the backdrop of warriors preparing for war.

"Mayhap." She stepped closer, placing her hands on Gita's shoulders. "But I need you here on Midgard."

Determination flashed in Gita's hazel eyes. "I won't hide in the mountains."

Brenna inclined her head, reluctantly acknowledging that her friend would not be swayed. "Will you wait in the great hall? If the town is breached and Gorm makes it this far, I would have you defend the wounded and my hall."

"We both know he will not make it that far, Valkyrie," replied Gita with a nod, the smile reaching her eyes.

"May the gods make it so."

AS THE AFTERNOON WORE ON, Brenna returned to the training yard and addressed her army. They had cleaned and prepared their weapons and shields, ready to defend their town and their lives.

"Warriors and shield maidens of Birca, today we will stand as one people, united against our common enemy," her eyes swept amongst the ranks assembled before her.

"Gorm, the Usurper of Gyldarhagi, would take Birca for himself. And make no mistake, our lives would not prosper under his rule, even if he forced me to rule at his side.

"We have made sacrifices to the All-father, to Tyr and to Thor; that their might and cunning will guide us in the battle that lies ahead of us."

She looked at the faces of her people and saw the strength of their resolve. Pride swelled inside her chest. It mattered naught that they were outnumbered, the people of Birca would not go down without a fight. And the gods willing, they would prevail.

"We will fight for Birca!"

A cheer went up.

"We will fight for our homes and our families."

The roar grew louder.

"The gods are with us!"

The battle cry filled the air, along with axes and swords, their blades glistening in the sunlight.

"For Birca!"

"For Jarl Brenna!"

May the gods make it so.

FROM INSIDE THE GREAT HALL, Brenna knew the shadows were beginning to draw longer outside.

"We cannot wait any longer." She took up her shield. Her sword and axe were strapped to her back; her hair braided into tight rows. She was ready to fight.

"It has not been two hours since the scout brought news of King Aric's army," said Torsten. The council had gathered in the great hall, along with the wounded.

"They won't be far," said Brenna. "I am confident my warriors can hold off Gorm's men in the meantime."

She read the worry in the faces of her council and intolerance for their fear surged to the surface. Once she had thought they feared her, now she could see they were weak men who feared everything that threatened their own comfort.

"If our lack of numbers concerns you, mayhap you will pick up a sword and fight for your Jarl." She lanced her gaze through each of them. "For your town and your people."

She channelled her disgust into her fist, landing it onto her shield as she spoke the name of the gods. "May Thor give us strength and courage, may Tyr give us battle luck and watch over our fight, may Odin give us battle wisdom and strength of strategy."

The four men of the council shrank back, colour draining from their faces. Gita came forward, dropping four swords at their feet. "There are shields at the door."

Brenna warmed at the strength and courage of her friend. When she had dispensed of Gorm, she would deal with her council. She stretched her neck to either side, and made for the beach.

Nearing her army, they parted to let her pass through.

"Thor is with us, Jarl," said one man.

"The All-father watches over us," said a shield maiden.

She nodded at each as she passed, letting their loyalty and courage add steel to her spine. *I am ready, Odin.*

On the beach, Gorm's men formed a line stretching from one end to the other, three warriors deep. Another group of twenty men stood behind them, along with the archers. The sun had begun its descent, leaving only two hours of sunlight in the day.

Gorm stood confidently at the head of his army. He was dressed in brown leather armour that had not a single scratch, embossed with gold chain and studs, over black trousers. An impressive black fur draped his shoulders, held in place with gold brooches and chain. His hair was washed clean of blood, and encircled with the thick, gold crown. He stood apart from his army, with only one man close by holding his shield and double-headed axe. His sword was sheathed across his back. She shuddered at the realisation that Gorm looked like a King.

Eric and Snorri called Birca's army to attention. A dozen

archers stood on higher ground on either side of the beach; another dozen waited behind the lines of Brenna's army. Birca had roughly half the number of warriors that stood behind Gorm. Still, they eyed the enemy with conviction - victory or Valhalla.

"At last," boomed Gorm as she approached him. "Have you been preparing our marriage bed?"

Laughter echoed from the ranks of his men standing behind him.

Brenna swallowed the repugnant taste the thought produced. She would rather die than lay with this pig.

"Neither Birca nor I will surrender to your demands." Her voice was strong and clear, carrying across the beach so all would hear. She would not bend to the will of this man.

The mirth transformed his smile into an evil grin. "Then you will join Odin in his golden hall tonight, Jarl Brenna. Birca will be mine - if not through bond, then through battle."

His men erupted into a bloodthirsty howl.

Brenna stood firm, letting the noise from the ranks of Gorm's swine wash over her. She believed in the army at her back; and she believed in the fate the gods had set out for her. Her gaze remained on the warmonger, as she felt Vali and Ivar come to stand on either side of her.

A battle horn sounded from the mountains behind the town, joined immediately by another from the mouth of the fjord.

"Aric," she whispered.

The battle cries on the beach hushed. Gorm's eyes flashed with anger.

Brenna cocked her head and she smiled up at her enemy. *Now I will make you bleed.*

11

*F*reshly sharpened blades caught the sun, reflecting like bolts of lightning sent by Thor before the blood rained down.

Two of Gorm's warriors stepped in front of him as he flung his fur at the man behind him.

Vali saw his own bloodlust reflected in the enemy before him. Now that the battle was inevitable, neither side much cared who had the greater numbers; their fates had already been set by the gods.

The roar of warriors launching into battle harmonised with the whistle of arrows and the beating of hooves and feet as Aric's army raced down the mountainside to join the fray. Axe and sword and bone clashed in a disjointed symphony of screams of the living and the dying.

All faded into the background, under Vali's breath and heartbeat; only the occasional roar of attack brought warning. For now, his sword remained sheathed on his back, favouring his axes outside of the shield wall behind him.

He spun and hacked, swinging his axes high and low. He sensed Brenna nearby, but his focus did not waver. He had learnt not to question her skill on the battlefield. Doing so would only get him killed; or worse - earn her wrath. She was the Valkyrie of Birca; she did not need him to defend her. Behind him, the shield wall would part periodically to let some of Gorm's warriors through. Once surrounded in hand to hand combat, he knew most would not survive.

"Vali!"

Brenna's voice cut through the melee. He turned to find her, then cast his gaze along with hers to the longboats. Four drakkars were moving away. Gorm was attempting to flee before Aric's boats reached the docks.

"Archers," he bellowed. "Stop those boats!"

At his command, warriors detached from the shield wall and set themselves on the much depleted enemy forces still on the beach. Vali worked his way towards the water, but it was no easy matter for the men Gorm left behind were determined to fight until the death.

Having no time to retrieve the axe lodged in the face of a Viking, he reached for his sword. Deflecting a blow from his right, Vali swung the second axe, slicing open the belly of his opponent. A bloody roar came from his left, the air swooshed above him as he ducked in time to miss the axe aimed at his neck. He thrust his sword, cutting along the thigh of the Viking as he raised his axe above his head. Vali pivoted, using the momentum to bring his own axe across his back, finally felling the man in one clean sweep.

Flames burst through the sky above him, heading towards the water. He watched in disappointment as those that hit the boats were quickly doused. No arrows were fired in return from the drakkars. Gorm's remaining men continued to fight hard, determined to die well.

"Kill them all!" came the call from King Aric, still mounted atop his horse.

Vali stretched his shoulders back. "Gladly," he muttered, raising his axe once more.

HE TOOK a long draft of ale, watching on from the edge of the village as Brenna's men walked amongst the sea of corpses. Their wounded had been carried back to a longhouse close to the great hall, and their dead were laid out and awaiting burial. He winced at the grunts that could be heard as spears were driven into enemy fighters still breathing. Killing in battle was one thing, but he had no stomach for the nasty aftermath of war.

Beyond the beach, villagers were already collecting wood and building the pyres that would burn their remains.

"Too much blood has been spilled on these shores in recent times."

Vali grinned at the familiar voice.

"Ragnar Eriksson. Well met, my friend!" Vali greeted the King's chief huscarl, who had once threatened to send him to Valhalla if he stood in the way of his daughter's marriage.

"And you, Vali Hrolfsson." They stood shoulder to shoulder above the carnage.

"Little of Birca's blood soaked the ground, this time."

Ragnar raised his drinking horn and tapped it against Vali's. "Praise be to the gods. Skal!"

"Skal."

Vali looked at the older man. Ragnar's brown hair, flecked with grey, hung over his shoulders, matching the long beard braided from his chin. His mail and leather armour, though well worn, appeared unmarked from the battle. There was barely a sweat on his brow.

"Did you see much of the battle, Ragnar?"

"Nei, only from afar. I watched the níðingr run away once he caught sight of the King."

Vali heard the bitterness in his voice as he spoke of the man responsible for the death of his wife's family.

"I had hoped today Gorm would feel my axe at his throat." Ragnar spat on the ground.

Vali shook his head. "It seems the gods had other plans. Do you think he will sail for Fornsigtuna?"

Ragnar shrugged. "It is possible. The King left thirty of his warriors behind." He tipped the horn back, draining its contents.

"Gorm's army was almost halved. I doubt he would prevail in Fornsigtuna."

Aric's longboats had pulled alongside the docks. The stryrimaor's of each gesturing to their crews as they began to debark.

Ragnar gave him a tight smile. "You must excuse me, Vali. I would see my wife as she comes ashore."

"Hertha is here?" He had never known Hertha to accompany her husband into battle.

"Ja, she refused to stay at home."

Vali nodded and downed his ale. He headed in the opposite direction from Ragnar, to the great hall. Brenna would be there by now, as would the King. He was eager to learn if they were to give chase to Gorm and put an end to his rule over Gyldarhagi. He had another reason as well. He'd lost sight of Ivar in the battle and if he lived; Vali was curious to see if the man remained in Birca or had fled with Gorm. As much as he wanted to trust Ivar as Brenna did, his gut insisted she had been misled.

. . .

VALI ENTERED the great hall and stood in the shadow of a wooden pillar surveying those gathered. All of the wounded had been moved to a longhouse and now the servants were busy setting the hall to rights. Pitchers of ale and mead sat on tables, but the drinking was subdued. Brenna sat beside the fire pit, cleaning her weapons while Aric paced up and down the opposite side. Members of Brenna's council stood huddled out of reach of her sword, but not the dark looks she sent in their direction. Eric and Snorri sat by the fire, drinking ale.

Vali clenched his fists at the sight of Ivar sitting calmly by the fire, drinking from his horn. The man may be playing the part of a loyal servant but he was involved in the attack somehow, Vali just knew it.

"How is it possible these men were living right under your nose, Jarl Brenna?" The King threw his hands in the air. "Plotting against you, and no one noticed?"

This time he gestured at the four men of the council. Vali shook his head in disgust at how weak these men were. Not one of them possessed the mettle of leadership.

"Sire, no one in Birca has spoken of Gorm," said Brenna, handing her weapons to Gita to store. "He has been raiding in the west for years."

"And yet he has developed an interest in Birca. Nei! In you."

Brenna shrugged. "I was merely a means to an end. Gorm's interest was always Birca."

Aric looked her up and down, suspicion in his stare. "Why now?"

"Mayhap you should ask Ivar that question, my King." Vali poured himself an ale as he watched for Ivar's reaction. Keeping his eyes on him, he went to stand by Brenna.

King Aric's face looked as if he had smelt a rotting pot of meat. "Vali Hrolfsson, you survived the battle, I see."

Vali smirked. "You sound almost disappointed."

Aric ignored the barb. "Ivar, is there something you can add to this conversation?"

Ivar raised his shoulders and held his hands out in submission. "Naught that is not already known, Sire."

"Yet Vali seems to be accusing you of more?" Aric gestured between the two of them.

"It has become his habit," agreed Ivar.

"A habit I'll not break." Vali knew Aric would never take him on his word alone. Yet he was determined to have his thoughts heard.

He felt Brenna stiffen beside him. "Why are you raising this again, Vali?" she hissed. "Do you bring proof of your claims?"

"My suspicions have not changed."

"It is naught but a petty jealousy."

Vali rolled his eyes but held his tongue. Jealousy was not at play here; his gut was sure Ivar was up to something.

King Aric looked at each of them. "Jarl Brenna, it seems your house is not in order."

"Sire?"

"Your plan to bring Sigurd the Black's men into your army has not been without complication."

"They fought well for Birca."

Vali grimaced internally. He should have known the King would use their difference of opinion to undermine Brenna. Aric was a petty man.

"Ja, they were content with a sword in hand and blood to spill," replied Aric. "But they had not settled into the town as you had wished."

"There have been some challenges," admitted Brenna.

Aric laughed and Vali could almost hear her teeth grinding in frustration.

"Oh, come now." Aric stroked his beard. "Your people were at each other's throats. A group of traitors were living here for months and your own council were prepared to see you married off to a warmonger that they would then swear allegiance to."

Vali almost choked on his ale. He watched as the faces of Torsten and the other councillors grew scarlet and tried to shrink themselves into the shadows cast from the fire pit.

Brenna straightened her shoulders. "King Aric, you made me Jarl of Birca after I earned my place-"

"Ja!" Aric's voice rose. "But I would have your loyalty - and the loyalty of your people."

"You are questioning my fealty?" Her voice was softer, but filled with a strength Vali knew came from deep within her.

"Nei, Jarl Brenna. But I am questioning the fealty of Sigurd's men."

A heavy silence filled every space in the hall. The King's question was not without merit, and everyone present knew it.

"Sigurd's men were warriors without kin or clan." Aric took a step closer to Brenna. "An oath given after the death of their leader is one that is easily broken."

Vali wanted to place his hand on Brenna's but knew the action would be perceived as stifling rather than supportive. She did not need him to rescue her.

"These men fought for me without question, King Aric. I believe they are loyal to Birca."

"Then they will not mind being asked to state their fealty to their Jarl and to their King for all to witness."

Vali could feel Brenna's anger simmering beside him,

matching his own. King Aric was placing her in an impossible situation. Forcing these warriors to kneel and pledge themselves to her - again - after fighting with and for the Valkyrie of Birca was an insult to their honour. But insulting the King's honour could be deadly.

"Should we not be giving chase to the usurper and putting an end to him while the odds are in our favour?" asked Brenna. The edge in her voice was as sharp as her blade.

"That is the crux of the matter," said Aric. "We do not know that the odds are in our favour. And we will not know this until I look each of these men in the eye and see where their fealty lies."

"But-"

"Nei!" the King's tone sparked with anger as he cut her off. "They will kneel."

The scrape of a chair broke the heated silence as Ivar rose to his feet and came before Brenna.

"I will speak with the men," he said in hushed tones meant for her ears only. "I will let them know it is the King who demands they kneel and pledge themselves to both of you."

Vali bristled at Ivar's impudence. Brenna did not need Ivar to rescue her either.

She placed a hand on Ivar's shoulder. "Thank you, but that won't be necessary."

Ivar's brow furrowed as he stepped back. Vali watched the determination set in across Brenna's features.

"King Aric." Brenna's voice projected across the hall. "I am Jarl of Birca and these are my men. I say they have proven their fealty with their swords."

Aric scowled at her. The silence began to suffocate the room.

"Insisting the men kneel will undermine the unity we have achieved today."

Vali agreed. Everyone had fought well.

"Sire," Eric stood and inclined his head. "The Jarl is right. At the moment, our warriors and shield maidens are as one."

Aric glared at the hersir.

"Very well," he said. "We will make a sacrifice to the gods that we have thus far prevailed against our enemies. Then, we will feast."

Aric turned on his heel and headed for the door, ending any further discussion.

Eric nodded to Brenna, then he and Snorri also departed, with Ivar not far behind them.

Vali stood, stretching the ache that comes from battle from his back. "It seemed Ivar was happy to create tension with his men and force them to kneel."

Brenna sighed. "Vali, you don't know what you are talking about."

"Why did he move so quickly to do the bidding of the King when he knew it would only cause problems?"

"He was trying to help."

Vali shook his head. He had no doubt Ivar was trying to help, but whose cause was he helping?

12

*B*renna banished the council from her sight, an order they were quick to follow.

"Vali, this cannot continue," she said once they were alone. "You cannot question Ivar's loyalty when he has done naught to warrant such accusations."

A muscle spasmed in his jaw, a sure sign he would not back down from the argument.

"If you would just listen-"

"Nei!" The anger and frustration she felt towards Aric was quickly doubling in size, thanks to Vali's interference. It simmered dangerously close to the surface, and despite her efforts on the battlefield, her body tensed for another fight. "I cannot see why you are so troubled by Ivar. He has done naught but support me."

Vali gave her a look heavy with condescension.

"Do not say it! Ivar has never once behaved as though he wants to be my bedmate." She held up her hand to stop Vali from speaking. "And even if he had, do you really think my heart so disloyal to you?"

Vali shook his head. "Brenna... you have often said you

do not wish to be the pawn of men and politics; however, you have played that game many times yourself."

She clenched her fists so as not to wrap her hand around the hilt of her sword. How dare he throw her past decisions in her face?

"And now you are Jarl," he continued. "You of all people know how those who seek power will trade in manipulation and deceit."

She drew in a deep breath and pushed her anger aside. Brenna understood what he was saying but she just could not see Ivar in that role. Why could he not trust her judgement? She couldn't discuss this any further.

"Where is my father?"

Vali turned to her, surprise replacing the look of consternation on his face.

"Aric would not travel without him. Have you seen him?"

"Ja, Ragnar is well."

Relief eased a little of the tension in her body.

Vali reached for a pitcher and filled a horn with ale. "He was going to meet Aric's drakkars as they docked. Hertha was aboard."

"Mother is here?" She ignored his offer to pour her a drink.

"That is what Ragnar said."

Brenna could not think of a time when her Mother had travelled into battle. After Hertha's uncle's throne was stolen and his family murdered by Gorm, she had avoided bearing witness to any more bloodshed. She frowned, why would she come to Birca in this instance?

"I must find them."

"I'll join you," said Vali.

"That is not necessary." Brenna raised her hand as she

moved towards the double doors of the great hall. She could do with some distance from Vali at this moment.

He made no comment, following a few steps behind her. *Of course, he does not listen to me.*

They made their way past the longhouse where the wounded were being cared for. Warriors and townspeople alike called their greetings and blessings to their Jarl. The mood was one of relief. While they had lost men in the battle the previous evening, including those trapped in the longhouse, most were relieved to have not suffered much worse in their second meeting with Gorm. Brenna thanked the gods for her people's fealty and trust in her to lead and protect them.

As the sun began its final descent, the docks and the beach were a hive of activity. The invading dead were still being removed and Aric's boats were unloading. Brenna caught sight of her father helping her mother debark. They were alerted to her presence well before she reached them thanks to her own people hailing her as she passed by.

"Daughter! Another fine victory for you and Birca." Ragnar's grin lightened some of the tiredness Brenna saw in his eyes.

"Thanks to you and the King's army," she stepped into her father's embrace, enjoying the familiar scent and warmth she'd known her whole life.

"It was as the gods willed it," said Ragnar.

"Indeed." She pulled free and turned to her mother. The streaks of white had thickened a little in Hertha's golden hair. The usual sparkle seemed lost from her blue eyes.

"Mother, are you well?"

"Ja, Daughter," said Hertha with a tired smile. "Travelling by sea did not agree with me so well." She held her arms open and Brenna moved into them.

"But look at you, my beautiful shield maiden," she touched her forehead to her daughter's. "Leadership suits you."

"I do not think the King would agree," she murmured, grateful to be in her mother's presence. "Come. Let me get you some refreshment."

She glanced at her father, catching the frown on his face. "The King is preparing a sacrifice to thank the gods for our victory today, and then we shall feast."

Hertha turned to greet Vali, who still hovered behind her. Brenna scowled at him, then linked arms with her mother and began to move towards the great hall. She noticed Hertha and Ragnar exchange a discreet look.

"I am surprised to see you here, Mother," she said as they walked back to the great hall.

"Surprised and happy, I hope."

"Of course," Brenna smiled. "Is all well at Fornsigtuna?"

"Ja, all is well." She swivelled her neck to address Vali who was walking with Ragnar behind them. "Vali, I spoke with your mother only yesterday. The farm is doing well and your nephew is thriving."

"That is wonderful to hear. Thank you, Hertha." Brenna noticed Vali brighten considerably at the mention of his family. She pushed him from her mind and pondered why Hertha had come to Birca.

"Tell me, Brenna, what changes have you made to your hall? Have you added more rooms?" Hertha squeezed Brenna's arm.

She went on to describe the building project that had extended the private quarters of the great hall. Rooms that would accommodate her parents and the King this evening. Behind them, Ragnar and Vali spoke of Vali's successful trade expedition. Frustration stabbed at her gut; with all the chaos, she and Vali had barely any chance to discuss Birca's trading future in depth. Once more, her plans were put on hold.

They reached the hall and Brenna called for refreshments. As her parents ate some cheese and bread, they were joined by others, giving Brenna no opportunity to talk further with her mother about her presence in Birca. With the sacrifice approaching, she excused herself to bathe and change from her battle armour. Despite her feeling that something was very wrong, she would need to wait until later in the evening to understand why Hertha had travelled to Birca in the midst of a battle.

BRENNA WALKED through the people until she was opposite King Aric, who stood in the centre of the clearing in front of the great hall with the gothi, Hervor. Both wore white cotton tunics that reached to the ground. Aric wore his crown, and on his brow was the rune for Tyr to symbolise victory and honour. A cow stood tethered to an altar made of rocks, on which sat a large bowl to catch the blood that would be spilled. Carved effigies of Thor, Tyr and Odin sat along the altar.

The King raised his arms towards the night sky and began.

"We give thanks to the gods who, in their wisdom, blessed us with a great victory over our enemy.

"Hail Thor, god of thunder and war. We give thanks for your strength to stand against those who opposed us.

"Hail Try, wise and strong one-handed god. We give thanks for your bravery in battle.

"Hail to Odin, wise and knowing All-Father. We give thanks for your wit as sharp as any sword, with judgment as deep as

any chasm, with strength to bear any misfortune. We honour your commitment to survival, your endless gathering of knowledge, and your unfaltering drive toward victory."

Hervor stepped forward and placed an axe into Aric's hands, reminding Brenna of the countless sacrifices she'd watched over the years, giving thanks to the gods for victory against their enemies, when she'd fought for Aric in Fornsigtuna.

The gothi moved around in front of the cow, holding its head still as she whispered prayers of thanks.

"Mighty Thor, Tyre and Odin. Accept this sacrifice of blood in thanks for our victory in battle."

The axe swung hard, slicing the cow's neck. Blood spattered Aric and Hervor, running into the bowl as the animal fell to its knees. Servants held the creature in place until the bowl was filled. Hervor lifted the bowl and poured the blood over each of the carved statues. A cheer went from the crowd gathered around.

"People of Birca. We have won a great victory. But it has not been without loss."

Brenna watched on as Aric moved his gaze over the people gathered.

"It seems there were those among you who sought to end the rule of your Jarl."

A murmur rippled through the people. They had not forgotten the traitors who had started this fight. Annoyance forced Brenna to straighten her shoulders and raise her chin. Where was Aric heading with this?

"The traitors responsible were new to Birca. They'd fought for Sigurd the Black. They'd raised their weapons against the people of Birca once before and failed. And when offered their freedom and a new start here in Birca, these traitors conspired against your Jarl, against your

King." Aric paused. "They conspired against the people of Birca."

Brenna glared at the King. He may not force the men to kneel, but he was still creating a division.

The crowd grew louder in agreement.

"Of course," said Aric. "This does not mean that all of those that came from Sigurd's defeated army are traitors. Nei, they fought beside you today. They fought for their Jarl and for Birca."

What game was Aric playing? What could he gain from undermining the newfound unity of her people? Mayhap Loki was whispering in his ear?

"Sire, you have our swords," called a voice from the crowd.

Aric gave a well-practised smile of false benevolence. "And I thank you for it".

"We fight for the Valkyrie of Birca," called another, and was met with agreement and cheers.

Smiling, Brenna felt the hand of Frigga at work.

The King looked as if he'd tasted something vile. He nodded once and took his leave.

Pleased that Aric had not persisted in trying to subvert her people against each other, Brenna stepped forward, needing to assure her people that she was grateful to them all.

"Birca! Your bravery and strength on the battlefield did not go unnoticed by the gods. You all fought well today. For Birca."

"For Birca!" came the resounding reply.

Brenna inhaled the confidence reflected from her people. She was the Jarl of Birca and, while some may try, none would succeed in usurping her authority. The gods had decreed it so.

13

While the people toasted the gods and their ancestors, the servants were busy roasting meats and boiling stews, preparing platters of buttered root vegetables, greens and sweet fruits and nuts. Pitchers of ale and mead sat on every table, and the great hall was filled to capacity.

Vali's mood had cheered considerably as he revelled in the victorious atmosphere in the hall. He sat at a table including Ragnar and Hertha, and Frode and Nissa. The women spoke of the baby growing in Nissa's belly, with Hertha sharing her advice as well as the experience of Aric's wife, Queen Ylva, who'd been safely delivered of a son just three months prior. Vali listened with half an ear, mindful of Ragnar's stony silence.

"Is something on your mind, Ragnar?"

The huscarl inhaled loudly through his nose, keeping his arms firmly folded in front. "Aric always does what is best for Aric."

Vali couldn't hide his surprise. Ragnar was, and had always been, Aric's man.

"We should be going after Gorm, not sitting here watching Aric feed his ego."

Vali didn't disagree. "So why are we sitting here, Ragnar?"

Ragnar studied the King. "That is a question I have never been able to answer."

Frode glanced over at him, eyebrows raised. Vali gave a slight shake of his head, wanting to hear Ragnar's point of view on the matter without interruption.

"For the second time, Aric has let Gorm go without consequence. Each time, there was every chance we would be victorious in battle," Ragnar's tone was slow and even.

Vali watched as a storm raged behind Ragnar's eyes. He understood all too well the frustration of his own advice falling on deaf ears.

"Yet he would not give chase, he would not confront Gorm and put an end to his tyranny," the huscarl said.

Vali stretched his mind back. He had helped defend Fornsigtuna from attack, and he had been on many of the raiding expeditions. But those raids were to bring back wealth, never to expand Aric's holdings.

"I thought Aric was content with his territory. Content with the level of responsibility the gods had bestowed on him," said Vali.

"If he had repelled Gorm all those years ago in Gyldarhagi, he would be King of all Svealand?" Frode looked between the men for confirmation.

"Nei," said Vali. "As cousin to Princess Ingrid, Hertha would have a claim."

"Hertha did not want the throne," said Ragnar quietly.

"Did the King know this?" asked Vali.

The older man turned to look him in the eye. "He did."

A thousand questions flooded his mind. What Viking

King would not take advantage of the opportunity to extend his territory and power? Or to avenge those wronged in times of war? Especially one who craved glory and recognition as much as Aric.

From the dais, Brenna rose to address the townspeople.

"People of Birca. Over the course of this day and this evening, we have grown stronger together. We are united as one. Let us give thanks to the gods for our combined strength and the feast we are about to have.

"Lord Odin and lady Frigga, we give our greetings to thee. We give thanks for our brothers and sisters. Bless this bounty set here before us. Hail and love to Odin and Frigga."

"Hail and love to Odin and Frigga," came the reply.

"Let us feast!" said Brenna to the cheers of the crowd. "Skal."

Vali raised his horn to her. She was still the headstrong, beautiful, intelligent, determined and infuriating girl he fell in love with all those years ago. She was as fierce a leader and protector of her people as she was a warrior. He may not always agree with her, but there was no other he would rather fight for, or along side.

He watched as Aric raised his own drinking horn. The King's smile, though carefully in place, did not reach his eyes. It was not Aric basking in the people's adoration, and Vali couldn't help but wonder who would suffer the consequences of this.

Vali made his way through the crowd to the main table to join Brenna for the meal. Ivar was already seated at the table, along with the members of the council. He grimaced, but held his tongue.

"Jarl," he murmured the greeting in Brenna's ear, hopeful she would not ignore his presence this time.

"Styrimaor." The corner of her mouth lifted. "You are new to this place. Mayhap you should pledge yourself to me?"

Desire stirred. "I believe I have already demonstrated my fealty by way of worship in your temple, Valkyrie."

Heat flooded Brenna's cheeks. "It never hurts to reaffirm oneself."

He chuckled. "As you wish."

"What are you two whispering about?"

"Nothing of consequence, Mother," said Brenna as she gestured for a servant to fill her drinking horn.

Hertha smiled knowingly at Vali and took her place beside Torsten.

Platters were presented to the main table and everything else was forgotten as everyone sated their hunger. Eventually, conversation began to flow again. Vali couldn't help but notice Ragnar's ongoing silence. He decided to ask the question most in need of an answer.

"So, King Aric, when do we sail in pursuit of Gorm?"

Aric licked the meat from his lips and took Vali's measure. "Why would we do that, Vali?"

"You think we should go after him over land?" He raised his eyebrows in mock innocence.

The King smirked in response. "It is clear our combined forces were enough to overcome Gorm and his army. The battle is won and winter is fast approaching. Let Gorm go and lick his wounds while we prepare for the coming season."

"While he's licking his wounds, he will also be gathering his strength; replenishing his forces," said Brenna. "I think we should attack while we know he is weak."

His Valkyrie saw the merit in seeking vengeance on the

warmonger now. Vali grinned, she was every bit the daughter of Ragnar.

"Do we know that?" asked the King. "Gorm may have allies from afar waiting to ambush us if we pursue him. Mayhap he would lead us into a trap."

"Or mayhap we would crush him, end any further threat to our people and retake the throne of Gyldarhagi," said Brenna, with enough force to cause the conversations of those closest to their table to fall silent.

"Nei," Aric waved his hand as if to dismiss the matter. "We can achieve that in spring if the gods will it. Gorm will not bother us before then."

Vali watched with disbelief. It was clear that if Gorm won Birca, he would be able to attack Fornsigtuna from both sides. Why risk that? For all they knew, Gorm could be storming Fornsigtuna as they sat here debating the matter. For that reason alone, the King's army should at least give chase. Aric's lack of action made no sense to Vali.

"I would not be so certain Gorm is finished with Birca." The steady timbre of Ragnar's voice cut through the smouldering tension.

Aric turned to him with malice in his eyes. "And what evidence do you have of that, Ragnar?"

"The boat Gorm used to escape passed close to the boat Hertha was travelling on," said Ragnar.

Hertha sat perfectly still, staring straight ahead.

"Many years have passed," murmured Aric, the hostility had slipped from his face.

The sudden change of attitude from Aric caught Vali by surprise. He watched as Brenna looked from the King to her mother. Ragnar placed his hand over his wife's.

"He recognised me," Hertha whispered.

"Mother, what do you mean?"

Vali sensed Ragnar's frustrations were about to take on a much greater significance.

"How do you know he recognised you?" asked the King.

"Our eyes met, and I could see he knew me." Hertha turned to face both Brenna and Aric. "Then he called out as his drakkar moved past ours."

Vali looked between Ragnar's pensive stare to Hertha's face, drained of colour. Instinctively, he reached for Brenna's hand, covering it with his own.

"What did he say?" asked Aric.

Hertha cleared her throat, but not the tremble in her voice and she repeated Gorm's words. "I see you, Princess Ingrid. And I will return for what is mine."

"By the gods…" Vali whispered as trepidation ran up his spine. Who exactly was Hertha?

---

14

*B*renna stood abruptly, acid churning in her belly. "Nei, we will not speak of this here." She spoke over the top of Hertha's head, unable to bring herself to look her mother in the eye.

Without further consideration, she walked across to the heavy curtain that separated the private quarters from the great hall. Once there, she continued past the entry to her sleeping quarters and into a corridor leading to a smaller room with table and stools. She stood, her back to the door, waiting for the others to join her.

Her mind remained frozen as her lips trembled. She could not consider what her mother had implied until she could hear it said plainly. Footsteps sounded. One entered, two; then finally a third person.

"Brenna, please let me explain."

She turned to face the room. Hertha, Ragnar, Aric and Vali stood around the table. She did not indicate that any should sit.

"Why did he call you Princess Ingrid? Do you look that much like your cousin?"

Hertha shook her head. "I do not. Hertha had hair as black as a raven and eyes as green as the forests."

Hertha? Brenna clenched her fists, studying her mother for signs of the woman she was describing. "But, you are Hertha."

"Brenna, there is much we have not told you," said Ragnar.

Her eyes darted to her father. His face was as ashen as her mother's. What secrets had they kept from her?

"I don't understand."

Her mother pulled a stool from the table. "Please, let's sit."

Vali came to her aid, pulling a stool free and guiding her to sit down. He sat beside her, her mother on the other side next to Ragnar, then the King. Her mother took her hand in her own.

"When Gorm came to Gyldarhagi, he showed no mercy. When my father, the King, called for a parley during the battle, Gorm tricked him. He took him captive and then blood eagled him in front of my mother and I, and all our people."

Brenna gasped as nausea tightened her belly. She had never heard this version. Tears pricked the back of her eyes.

"As my father breathed his last agonising breath, Gorm slit my mother's throat so my father would see her die."

A fire born of fury swept over Brenna's skin. She squeezed her mother's hand.

"Gorm took me prisoner while the battle continued."

Brenna looked to her father. His jaw was set hard, his fists clenched on top of the table. She could see the rage throbbing in his veins. Her own anger hardened into cold fear.

"But the King arrived and Father found you, he saved you..." Brenna's voice wavered.

"Ja, Ragnar saved me."

She turned to Aric. "Why did you not kill Gorm and retake the throne for her. She is the rightful heir and Queen?"

"There is more to this story, Brenna," said Aric gently.

She looked back to her mother.

"When I was his prisoner," A distant look came over her face, as though she had barricaded her true self away. "Gorm used me as he saw fit. He broke my spirit and my body."

The bile rose in Brenna's belly, the blood in her veins turning to ice. She wanted to place her hands over her ears and block the words coming from Hertha's mouth.

"He wanted me as his Queen. Despite slaughtering my parents and my people, he believed this would bring legitimacy to him." Bitterness stole into her voice. "He thought I would thank him, admire him..."

Cruel images taunted Brenna as she watched her mother fade even further into her memories.

"When Ragnar found me, I was all but dead. I wanted to die."

She came back into herself and looked Brenna in the eye. "I swore I would never be his Queen."

Brenna saw her mother's fierce determination, a trait she recognised in herself. It closed around the pain, trapping it inside a steel cage.

"I'm sorry," said Vali. "I cannot imagine what you have lived through. But I do not understand, how did Gorm survive the battle once the King's army arrived?"

She became aware of Vali rubbing circles on the small of

her back with the palm of his hand, and she thanked the gods he was here beside her.

Ragnar shifted in his seat, hostility appeared to radiate from every bone in his body. Brenna knew he had as much cause as Hertha to hate Gorm and wish for his death.

"We came to support King Haldor," said Aric. "By the time we arrived, Gorm had killed him and Queen Runa and taken the throne. The fighting was brutal and we faced the certainty of losing more than we could gain."

Rassragr!

"You did not fight to avenge the deaths of Haldor and Runa?" asked Brenna, with steel in her voice.

"The gods were not with us that day," replied Aric.

Brenna swallowed the acid in her throat. How could he not try to defeat the war monger, especially as he would be right next to his own border?

"The King struck a deal with Gorm," said Ragnar. "He could keep the throne of Gyldarhagi so long as he did not invade Aric's lands."

Brenna heard the resentment in her father's voice. "Is that true?"

"I saw what Gorm had done to the people of Gyldarhagi, I could not allow my own people to face such a fate."

There was silence in the room. The King looked resolute, with no sense of remorse for his actions. No doubt, thought Brenna with disgust, Aric did not want to face the possibility of meeting the same fate as King Haldor.

Her mother sat very still beside her; head bowed.

"Mother," Brenna squeezed the hand that still held hers, "if you are Princess Ingrid, why did you take on your cousin's identity?"

Sadness tinged the small smile on her lips. "Hertha was my dearest friend. When Gorm came for me, she stood in his way. He cut her down without a second thought." She shook her head. "I thought if the gods saw fit to keep me alive, I could not do so as a princess without a kingdom; and I had no desire to be Queen and see more blood spilled in my name."

"So, father married you as Hertha to complete the ruse?"

"In a way, ja..." Her mother glanced up at Ragnar with unshed tears.

Her father's anger seemed to have been replaced with a heaviness that made no sense to Brenna. She looked to each of her parents as an unspoken conversation played out between them. Hertha placed her hand on Ragnar's face, her thumb caressing his cheek. He covered her hand with his own.

"Brenna," he began. "I have raised you and loved you as only a father can."

Fear as sharp as any dagger raced up her spine. The deep timbre of Ragnar's voice carried a melancholy unfamiliar to her.

Her mother's grasp tightened on her own hand. *Gorm and her mother?* Brenna did not want to hear any more.

"Do not say it," she whispered. Hearing the words out loud would make it real. This could not be true.

"I carried you in my womb before Ragnar rescued me," said Hertha.

Brenna shook her head. She would not believe she could be a child conceived in violence and terror. A child with the same blood as Sigurd and Gorm.

"I'm sorry," her mother whispered.

"Nei, I cannot be his child." Anger, terror and disbelief raced through her body, sending a sickening heat all over and threatening to erupt as her stomach heaved.

15

"By Thor's blood," whispered Vali in shock.

Brenna rose, wrenching her hand from her mother's. She seemed not to hear the pleas of Ragnar and Aric to listen; nor of Hertha telling them to give her time as she rushed from the room.

"I will go," he said, recovering himself enough to go after her.

When he reached their chamber, he found her staring at the shield on the wall. It was painted green, with the rune symbolising heritage painted in black across it. This was the shield Brenna had adopted when she became Jarl of Birca.

"Who am I?" she whispered. "Everything I have known is lies."

He came to stand behind her, lightly touching his hands to her arms.

"I know who you are."

She sank back against him.

"You are Brenna Ragnarsdotter. The most stubborn woman I have ever met."

She grunted and placed her hand over his.

"You are a fierce shield maiden; protector of your people."

He wrapped his arms around her.

"The Valkyrie of Birca."

He pressed his lips against her hair.

"This shield... it's who I thought I was meant to be."

Vali followed her gaze. "You were destined to rule, Jarl Brenna."

"The blood of Gorm runs through my veins."

He felt her body shake, her muscles clench as she fought for control.

"The blood of Kings and Queens runs through your veins."

She turned in his arms. "I do not feel any connection with that monster."

"Why would you? You were raised by Ragnar and Hertha."

He'd known this woman her whole life. She had not a single trait of Gorm. She looked like her mother; fought like her father.

"Even standing face to face with him, I sensed nothing." Her anxious eyes searched his.

He took her face in his hands. "You are Brenna Ragnarsdotter, Jarl of Birca. You may have been conceived by force, but you were born in love."

He smoothed her hair back from her brow. "The gods chose you for this fate."

"Mayhap." She pulled away from him and went to stand by the fire.

Vali spied a pitcher of mead on the side table. He poured a cup for each of them, then came to stand beside her. Her brow was furrowed and the flames from the pit reflected in her eyes.

He handed her the mead. "What are you thinking?"

She shook her head and took a sip of mead. "I think the shock is wearing off a little."

He watched her as she moved the pieces of the puzzle in her mind.

"And I am angry."

He took a long swallow of his drink, savouring the velvety sweetness while he waited for Brenna to order her thoughts. He had never known her to fall prey to her emotions, preferring to apply logic and calm to any problem she faced.

"Why did they not tell me the truth?"

Vali had no answer.

"Why tell me now?"

"If Gorm knows Ingrid lives and that she bore a child... mayhap they wanted you to hear the truth from them rather than suspicions and half-truths from him on the battlefield."

She began to pace in front of the fire pit. "And Aric! What kind of King allows another to be blood eagled without cause and does naught to avenge the injustice?"

Vali pulled a stool close to the pit and took a seat. He'd had the same thoughts.

"Truly the gods were not with the people of Gyldarhagi if their ally turns tail without barely drawing a sword in their defence."

The agitation increased in her voice in time with her pacing. The fire burning in her eyes now came from within.

"And why does Aric not go after Gorm now? What is he afraid of?"

Vali could think of only one reason, but it was unfathomable. "Losing?"

She stopped and turned to him. "Ja, that is it." She

closed the distance between them. "Aric has never taken up a fight he cannot win."

He swallowed hard. They may be speaking the truth, but it was also verging on treason. The King would not tolerate such talk. He stood and took her hand in both of his.

"Brenna, you are right to be angry. But consider your words. Aric is our King."

The fire in her eyes still burned, but she held her tongue, gently removing her hand and returned to her pacing.

"Will you speak with Ragnar and Hertha tonight?" He took his seat once more.

She shook her head. "Nei."

He said no more. He wanted to understand but he knew it was impossible. Ragnar and Hertha had always loomed large in Brenna's life. And now neither were who she thought they were.

"I am tired and angry and... unsure of my place..." She stopped walking, raising a hand to rub her forehead. "I would drink my fill of mead but I need a clear head."

Vali rose to his feet, thinking to rub the pain from her temples and soothe some of her anguish away.

"Where is Ivar?"

He stopped in his tracks. "Why?"

"I wish to know his thoughts on launching an attack on Gorm tomorrow."

Tension knotted his shoulders. Could they get through one discussion without Ivar?

"It is late and the warriors are full from the feast and drunk from ale. Now is not the time to plan for battle."

Brenna scrubbed at her face.

"And you are tired. Come." He reached for her hand. "Let's get some rest. It will all be waiting for you tomorrow."

He grasped her hand in his, relieved when she did not resist, and led her to the fur-covered bed. Kneeling before her, he removed her soft leather boots. Small braids held her hair back from her face. With gentle hands, he began to loosen them, combing his fingers through long locks. She wore a velvet dress, the same shade of green as her shield. The shoulder straps untied with one pull, and he slipped the fabric down her arms and over her hips, letting it pool at her feet.

Reaching behind her, he pulled the fur coverings down so she could climb inside. Several candles were lit around the bed chamber. Vali walked to each, snuffing them out between his fingers. The fire provided a warm glow. Removing his boots and clothes, Vali joined her in the bed.

"This anger sits like a stone in my belly."

He traced a finger along her jawline. Dark shadows sat beneath eyes that flickered with both fury and injury. He placed a kiss on her forehead.

"When I was a small boy and something had angered me, my mother would stroke my head and kiss me here," his lips pressed against her forehead again, "and somehow the anger would start to fade."

She raised an eyebrow at him. "That is all it takes?"

"When I was but five summers in age, ja." He smiled at her.

"You think I am behaving as a child?"

He rubbed his nose against hers. "Nei, I think the child in you is hurting while the woman rages."

Brenna sighed. "What can I do?"

"Tonight," he pulled her close so her head rested against his shoulder, "you can do nothing except sleep and trust that the gods will show you the way."

16

_B_lades crashed and axes swung in slow motion. Each hit vibrated across the landscape and through her bones. Brenna sliced and hacked her way through enemy Vikings, but none would raise their sword for a lethal blow against her. She looked around and could see none of her warriors. She called for Vali and Ivar; for Eric and Snorri. She received no reply. She looked for her father. Surely, he would not leave her alone on the battlefield?

"Ragnar?" her voice rose above the melee.

"Daughter! He is here."

The voice that answered was familiar, although it was not her father's. The fighting had stopped. Warriors stood aside, forming a passageway. What magic was at play here? Gripping her weapons, Brenna moved in the direction of the voice. Her heart beat a steady march, as loud as Thor beating his anvil. She wanted to run, but her feet refused to hurry.

"Brenna," rasped the voice she knew to be Ragnar. "Come no further. You must leave this place."

"Father?" Something was wrong. She pushed harder against the invisible force determined to maintain her slow progress down the long corridor of warriors, blood still dripping from their swords.

Finally, she reached a clearing.

"Brenna, no."

She gasped. Ragnar was on his knees, shirtless with his arms tied to a post on either side. Behind him, King Aric stood dressed in a long white tunic and holding a long blade and a small axe. She had never witnessed such an execution but she knew Aric meant to blood eagle her father.

"Daughter, you have arrived," boomed the voice again.

The sound of her own breath filled her head as she turned to find Gorm, dressed as finely as any King in a black leather tunic and trousers, with his massive black fur across his shoulders. Beside him, dressed in a rich red gown with a steel collar at her throat, was her mother. Gorm held the chain attached to her collar in his hand. Silent tears fell down her face.

"It was a trap," Brenna whispered.

"Come, mighty shield maiden and rightful Princess of Gyldarhagi." Gorm held out his hand, gesturing for her to join him and Hertha.

Instead, she turned to Aric. "What are you doing? Ragnar is your friend, your chief huscarl. Why would you kill him?"

Aric held her in his steely gaze, giving no reply.

"Ragnar Eriksson," said Gorm, "is guilty of stealing my Queen and my child; he is guilty of keeping them hidden all these years. For that, he must die."

"King Aric, you cannot do this," she pleaded.

"Please, Aric," cried Hertha.

"Brenna, you must run," said Ragnar. "This is not your fate."

Aric placed the axe on the ground, stepping closer he raised the blade to Ragnar's spine at the top of his shoulders.

Her scream filled the space. Strong hands held her as the vision disappeared.

"Brenna! You are dreaming, wake up!"

Her chest heaved ragged breaths. "Ragnar... I must save him."

"Brenna!"

She looked around. She was in her bed with Vali at her side. Relief collided with her fear.

"A dream?" she whispered.

"Ja," said Vali, stroking her hair.

She let him pull her down under the furs, his arms wrapping around her. The memory of the dream left her trembling. She could not allow her father to suffer the same fate as her grandfather. When the morning came, she knew what she must do.

BRENNA ROSE BEFORE THE SUN. Vali barely stirred as she slipped from his arms. She stoked the fire and dressed quickly, leaving her hair flowing free. She walked quickly through the private chambers and across the great hall. The fire burned high in the oblong pit; the servants appeared to be the only other people awake.

The predawn light shrouded the town, turning buildings into formless shadows; the waning moon barely lit her path. Her breath hung in the frigid air, a warning that winter was only weeks away. Brenna made her way through the marketplace and past the longhouses, towards the mountain.

This was not where her townspeople had hidden when Gorm attacked; those mountains sat behind the great hall and could be accessed through a series of trails that led to the caves. The mountain cave Brenna headed for sat above a wall of stone. The climb was hard going, the ledges small and easily missed. Thankfully, the sun had begun it's slow ascent by the time she began her climb, making the task slightly less daunting.

It was only the second time she had made this journey, but she knew the higher she went, the easier it would become with the rocky ledges growing in size and the incline decreasing until it became flat enough to walk upright the remainder of the way.

At the top, Brenna looked out across Birca. Smoke rose from the longhouses, and further out, from the smaller houses. Servants scurried about their chores as the townspeople began to emerge and begin their day. The fjord stretched out between the mountains that guarded the port; the sun's rays not yet strong enough to light the kaleidoscope of colour that lay beneath the water's dark surface. The beach still held the scars of the recent battles.

She breathed in the clean, fresh air, letting it cleanse her from the inside out. By staying focused on reaching her destination, Brenna had kept her thoughts tightly bound. But now she must face the ugly truths revealed to her. She needed to make sense of what it meant.

Turning back towards the mountain, she walked alongside the boulders until she found the opening she sought. She had arrived at the home of Einar, the ancient one.

The warm fingers of fire beckoned from within. She felt her way through the narrow passage until it opened into a small cave. Naught had changed since Brenna had last been here. Bones and feathers were scattered and placed as protection and offerings to the gods. Skins and furs lay piled up on which he slept. As always, the Seer sat beside his fire pit.

"Jarl Brenna, I see the gods have revealed more of their secrets."

"It is a knowledge I did not welcome."

He gestured for her to sit, and she sank onto the ground opposite him. Beneath the black linens that covered his head and body, she could only see the bottom of his face; flesh as pallid as grey moonlight and a mouth darkened by kohl, or age, or both.

"Ancient one, did you know who my mother was? My father?"

"The gods pick and choose what they share with me. That you were the daughter of Ragnar Ericsson and his wife Hertha? I only saw that there was more to be revealed."

"And now you know?"

"I know what you know, shield maiden."

Tears rose unbidden, her anger usurped by hurt. "Why was it kept from me? Did my mother not trust me to keep her secret safe?"

"That is not a question for me or the gods."

She rubbed away a tear that had escaped down her cheek.

"What is the question you really want to ask?" Spittle shone on his yellowed teeth as he pulled his mouth into a mirthless smile.

Wrapping her arms around her waist, she shook her head. "I feel as though my past has been erased. I do not know who I am, or who I am supposed to be."

"Naught has changed."

"Everything has changed!" The depth of her words stole her breath. If she was not the daughter of Ragnar and Hertha, but of Gorm and Ingrid, what did that make her?

"Valkyrie, is one lie enough to undo all of your truths?"

"I don't know," she whispered.

Einar picked up his collection of bones and rune stones, shuffling them in his bony hands.

"Do you remember the prophecy the gods bestowed upon you?"

Her brow furrowed in confusion. "Of course. They told me I would heal the scars of the past and rule in place of the ancestors."

"Not *the* ancestors, Valkyrie, *your* ancestors." He threw the bones and runes into the dirt. "The throne of Gyldarhagi has long called you."

Anger sparked inside her once more. "I could never claim the throne as Gorm's heir."

"Gorm is not the only King of whom you are heir." He ran his hands over the pieces in front of him; his head lifted towards the gods as if it would aid in hearing them whisper to him. "Your fate is bigger than you could ever imagine, Valkyrie. But it will not come without cost."

Brenna felt a chill in her bones, despite the warmth of the fire.

"What does that mean?"

"Loyalties will be tested and lost."

Images from last night's dream clouded her vision, and fear clutched her heart once more. "Whose loyalties, ancient one, tell me?"

He shrugged. "Our destiny is determined by our actions, but that which is fated must remain so. It is the way of the gods."

"The gods speak in riddles which make no sense."

"The gods speak what needs to be spoken." Einar held out his palm, ending the discussion

Swallowing her frustration, Brenna took his hand and with her tongue, licked from Einar's fingertip to wrist.

All-father, god of gods. Help me make sense of this. Help me understand who I'm supposed to be.

All she heard was a deafening silence.

17

*T*he stirrings of others outside the bedchamber woke Vali from his sleep. He stretched his hand across the bed, feeling only the soft furs by his side. Sighing in resignation, he stared at the timber beams above him. He hoped Brenna had gone in search of her mother, but experience suggested she would be keeping her mind busy with preparations for war, or other business within her jarldom. His Valkyrie was not prone to long bouts of self-pity.

Throwing the furs back, he rolled to the edge of the bed and sat. Mayhap he could be helpful, in whatever her endeavours entailed. He washed his face and dressed, placing a blade in his belt - in uncertain times he did not want to be unarmed.

It was still very early and there were not many people in the great hall except for servants and a forlorn looking Ragnar. Their relationship had certainly improved since Brenna became jarl, although the depth of it was yet to be tested. Vali took a deep breath and joined him at one of the long tables.

"Well met, Ragnar."

"Ah, Vali," he gave him a sidelong glance. "Well met."

"Is Hertha still abed?" He hoped Ragnar would tell him Brenna was with her mother.

"Ja, she did not sleep well." Ragnar's tone was heavy, his shoulders slumped.

"Nor did Brenna."

He grunted. "It is unlike her to stay sleeping so long."

"She's not," shrugged Vali. "She rose well before me."

Ragnar gave him a half-smile.

Gita appeared with bowls of stew and set one each in front of them. Vali nodded his thanks. He knew better than to ask Gita for Brenna's whereabouts. She would share the information if it was necessary. Her saying nothing was evidence that Brenna was well. His stomach grumbled so he concentrated on the food in front of him.

After a few moments of eating, Ragnar spoke. "She is angry."

Vali considered the statement. "I think confused is more accurate."

The older man turned to him. "What is Brenna confused about?"

"Who she is."

"She is who she always was."

"Ja, to you and I. But she has lived her life believing Hertha is her mother and Ragnar is her father. Now, Hertha is Princess Ingrid and Gorm's blood runs through her veins."

Ragnar inclined his head and sighed. "That is true. Mayhap I am the only one who feels that loss as well."

Vali's brow creased, not sure of Ragnar's meaning.

"For more than twenty summers, I have been husband to Hertha and father to Brenna. What am I now? Other than the King's fool."

"Ragnar! You and your daughter must learn to hold your

tongue." Vali glanced around the hall to ensure their conversation was not overheard.

"Aric is afraid of Gorm. He is afraid of losing his kingdom," Ragnar retorted.

"He has allies."

"Ja, but he lacks conviction."

Vali pushed his empty bowl away. "The Ragnar I know would do anything to protect his family. Has that changed?"

"Nei!"

"So why are you sulking, and speaking words that whisper of treason?"

The brief spark of passion in his eyes was replaced with an all-consuming pain. "What if I've already lost them?"

Vali placed a hand on the older man's shoulder, his fear resonating far more than he wanted to admit. "After everything you have done - all of your sacrifices - I cannot believe the gods would allow that to be your fate."

Ragnar looked him in the eye and gave a slow nod.

The doors of the great hall swung open, a cold breeze barely keeping pace with Brenna and Ivar. They both wore a look of determination. A third man followed close behind.

Vali felt his right eye twitch. It would have been easier all round if Ivar had fallen in the last battle.

"Where is King Aric?" called Brenna, sending servants scattering.

Vali and Ragnar rose.

"What is the matter?" asked Vali.

"We must go after Gorm. He cannot be allowed to hold the throne of Glydarhagi a moment longer," said Brenna, removing the fur that covered her shoulders. Her cheeks wore the glow of the morning chill and her eyes were shining with resolution.

As much as he might agree, Vali wanted to know what

had brought this sudden declaration of intent about. Or whom?

"That may be true, but how do you plan on convincing the King that we should strike now?" asked Vali.

"Jarl Brenna, I believe you summoned me?" King Aric stood at the entrance to the private quarters.

"We must talk," she said, ignoring the derision in his tone.

She and Ivar joined Vali and Ragnar at the table. Once Aric was seated, the rest of them did so, including the stranger who had entered the great hall with Brenna.

"Besides his attack on Birca, Gorm is mistreating his people," she said.

Aric raised an eyebrow. "What do you know of the people of Gyldarhagi?"

"Only what this wanderer has shared with Ivar and I." She gestured to the man at the end of the table. "This is Egil of Gotland. He recently travelled through Gyldarhagi and was shocked by what he saw there."

The King turned his gaze upon the wanderer. "I had heard that Gyldarhagi had prospered these many years thanks to Gorm's countless raiding parties to the west."

"That is true, King Aric. The success of Gorm's raids can be seen in the grandeur of his hall, the many boats he commands and the loyalty he buys from his warriors. But few come to his shores to trade, leaving his people to survive with what they grow on their farms or fish from the ocean. Many are hungry and they suffer with no support from their King, especially the elderly and those families whose husbands and fathers have gone on to Valhalla in service to their King."

Aric drummed his fingers on the table. Vali knew the King would be searching for more excuses not to attack.

"Tell me, wanderer," said Vali. "Did you hear any talk of jarls or kings who may be allies to Gorm?"

Egil shook his head. "Gorm is feared by all and his fortress near impenetrable. He has not had need to collect allies."

"And his army? What do they number?" asked Ragnar.

The wanderer shook his head. "I could not say for sure. There are always many warriors in Gyldarhagi, and he has four jarldoms under his command as well."

"So, he has some reserves waiting for him." Aric's tone suggested he was still not convinced.

"But he is returning with a depleted force," said Brenna.

Aric scratched his head. "Even with our armies combined, we were lucky to drive Gorm from Birca. I do not think we would be so lucky on his own land."

Vali frowned. He felt there had been a little more than luck at play on the battlefield.

"We call for allies." Brenna sat up straighter. "Gorm is feared by so many - there must be those who would stand with us to defeat him. Certainly, those loyal to King Haldor and his family."

"If it was known that Princess Ingrid lived-" began Ivar.

"Nei," Vali's temper flared. "What do you know of Princess Ingrid?"

"I have told Ivar the truth." Brenna's gaze locked on Vali.

The silence was filled with tension. Vali felt the muscle twitch in his jaw. She'd confided in Ivar? Is that who she'd crept out of their bed to see?

"Princess Ingrid died in the great hall of Gyldarhagi," growled Ragnar.

"Actually," said Aric. "I believe there is merit in what Ivar is suggesting.

A fist of steel curled tight in Vali's gut. Of course he would change his mind when it suited him.

"We should send word to our allies and those we believe sympathetic to this battle. Princess Ingrid, the rightful heir of Gyldarhagi lives and is ready to reclaim her throne."

Vali could feel the rage radiating from Ragnar. He put his hand on his shoulder, as much to still him as to show his support.

"I believe my mother should be consulted on this matter." Brenna's lips were tight; her jaw stiff.

"Nei," said Aric. "*I* am the King of *all* these lands. If we are to attack Gorm, it will be with the allies of both my Kingdom and the heir of Gyldarhagi."

Brenna's indignation at having her own words twisted and thrown back at her was palpable. From the look on Aric's face, his mind was made up. Ingrid would rise from the ashes - whether by choice or by decree appeared to be irrelevant. Vali's opinion of the King had been tarnished when he'd separated him from Brenna, insisting she marry Jarl Beinersson. But it now plunged to a new low.

"I have one request," said Brenna, holding Aric in her stare. "Gorm cannot know of my parentage. It will only fuel his determination to claim my mother as his Queen."

Aric lifted one corner of his mouth, his eyes remaining hard. "Of course, Jarl Brenna."

Vali could not tell if Aric could be trusted on this matter.

"Then it is decided. We will fight," said Brenna.

Vali saw the twisted smile on Ragnar's face. He may not agree with them using Hertha in this way, but given the opportunity, Vali was sure Ragnar would not be so fast to let Gorm escape for a third time.

18

*W*ith the King agreeing to attack Gorm, Brenna excused herself to go and check there would be horses available for the riders Aric would send out to his allies. In truth, she was not yet ready to speak with Ragnar. Nor had she missed the look on Vali's face when she'd returned to the great hall with Ivar. She could do without another pointless argument over Ivar's loyalty.

There was also a much more fraught issue to contend with. She had no doubt Ragnar would inform her mother about the King's decision. And that Hertha would not consent to her role in the plan. The King would order it done, regardless, but Brenna did not wish that burden on her mother if she remained so opposed to it. Mayhap there was another way? She would think on it and hope the gods provided a solution.

The village was completely awake with traders unpacking their wares at the marketplace and servants working through their tasks. Smoke plumed from every chimney and fishermen were returning with the morning's catch. Pride bloomed in her heart at the way her people focused on their future rather than dwell on their wounds.

Brenna slowed her steps as she approached the burnt out long house. Twenty men had been inside, unable to escape the flames. Four men were at work, shovelling and shifting debris. She recognised them as newcomers.

"Good morning, Jarl," said one when he saw her watching them.

"Well met, Jarl," said another.

"Well met,' she greeted them. "Have you volunteered for this work?" With everything that had occurred in the last few days, she had not found time to order the clearing of the destroyed building.

"Ja, Jarl," replied the first man. "Our brothers were inside. We wanted to make sure they had a proper burial."

A sense of shame heated her cheeks. She had been thoughtless to overlook this matter.

"What is your name?"

"I am Hroarr, and this is Amund, Torkel and Radalfr."

Brenna nodded at each of them. "Have you selected a place for their burial?"

"Nei, Jarl. Although we had hoped to find a place on top of that mountain." Horarr gestured to the mountain behind the great hall.

"Very fitting," said Brenna. "Their sacrifice helped to warn us and save our townspeople who were able to hide in the caves beneath the mountains. These warriors will be closer to the gods while they continue to watch over Birca."

They grinned their agreement.

Brenna picked up a shovel. "With your permission, I would like to help?" She looked to each of them again.

"Thank you, Jarl."

She threw herself into the work, glad to have a task that

took her thoughts away from Aric, Gorm and her mother. The horses would be seen to by one of the King's huscarl.

The larger pieces of charred wood had been neatly stacked to the side. Brenna worked side by side with the men to load the blackened wreckage of men and hearth into a cart. One by one, other warriors and villagers came to help. An atmosphere of silent camaraderie settled on them.

As the sun rose to the highest point in the sky, their work was done. Brenna sent a boy to the stables to bring some horses to take the cart to the foot of the mountain.

"Tonight, we will send these warriors on to Valhalla," she said to the people gathered.

"Jarl, we will find a place for the burial mound," said Hroarr.

Many voices added their desire to help.

A veil of calm had descended over Brenna, quieting some of the turmoil in her mind. This was the Birca, Brenna knew. These people didn't need to kneel to prove their fealty. She thanked each of them as she took her leave. Needing to hang on to this inner peace for a while longer, Brenna continued on to the paddocks where the horses roamed.

One of Tarben's innovations, when he'd been Jarl, had been to build a fence around a large parcel of land to keep the horses in one place where they could be tended to, and easily rounded up when needed. Elof had been a fierce warrior, fighting alongside Tarben in many battles. He'd lost his arm, and his eye, in a battle and could no longer fight. Tarben built a cottage for Elof and his family inside the paddock, leaving the horses in their care.

"Hail Elof," called Brenna, approaching the man as he stroked the back of one of his charges. "How did you fair over the last few days?"

"The Valkyrie herself has come to visit us," said Elof. "Well met, Jarl Brenna."

As Tarben's wife, Elof had barely acknowledged her. It appeared that hearing of Brenna's prowess on the battlefield had warmed him towards her.

Elof had his long grey hair plaited in one braid down his back, matching his braided beard. He did not cover the scar that crossed over the space where his left eye once was, often saying that the horses didn't care what he looked like. The right sleeve of his tunic was folded and tucked into his vest. The rest of him was still impressive.

"We were safe from the fighting. The horses kept themselves at the far boundary and I would have set them free if they'd looked in danger."

"Thank the gods our enemies did not get this far." Brenna reached up to scratch between the ears of the horse at Elof's side. "Are your wife and children well?"

"Ja, although my eldest boy was itching to join the fight."

"How old is Leif? Thirteen summers?"

"Ja, he believes he is too old to be running around with his younger brother and sisters."

Brenna grinned; she could remember her own impatience to face a real battle when she was a similar age. Out of the corner of her eye, she spied Lief listening to their conversation as he saddled a horse.

"I will not take him with us this time, but I do need young warriors to remain in Birca and protect the town," she said loud enough for Leif to hear.

Elof inclined his head in thanks before speaking again. "We have sent off four riders already this morning on the order of King Aric."

"Hoping to bring allies to our cause."

"Is it true, Jarl," asked Elof, his remaining eye squinting

at her. "Princess Ingrid of Gyldarhagi lives? That she is your mother?"

Aric had wasted no time in spreading the news of her mother's identity. She wondered if Hertha even knew of the plan yet?

"Ja, Elof. It is true."

"And she will reclaim the throne?"

Another horse approached, nickering softly for attention from Elof.

"Gorm must be defeated, and the King believes more of our allies will rally knowing that the rightful heir is alive." In truth, Brenna had no idea what her mother wanted to do. She gave Elof a tight smile. "Aric's army brought many horses with them. Please let me know if you need any extra help?"

"I think all the horses appreciate the extra bodies when the evening chill sets in," he chuckled, rubbing the second horse's neck.

Brenna gave the first horse a final pat and said goodbye to Elof, waving to the ever-attentive Leif.

The calm that had kept everything else from rising to the surface had evaporated. Word was spreading of Hertha's true identity. The time had come, she could no longer put off this conversation with her mother.

BRENNA DECIDED to bypass the great hall, and any further discussion with King Aric, entering through the kitchen. The servants bowed their heads respectfully as she passed by. Featherless chickens waited on a bench to be roasted for the evening meal, next to rows of bread rising under linen.

Gita met her in the passageway. "Jarl, you are a sight. I'll bring a pale of warm water for you to wash?"

Brenna looked at her hands, thick with blackened mud. "Thank you, Gita."

She walked a little further until she came to her bed chamber, relieved to find the room empty. It seemed she was making a habit of avoiding difficult conversations. Vali was determined to raise his suspicions of Ivar at every opportunity. She could not understand why Vali disliked him so much. She knew within herself that Vali was not jealous of Ivar. Yet he would not accept Brenna's word that he was loyal.

The curtain shifted and Gita appeared with the pale of water and a clean linen. Brenna dipped into the water and began removing the dirt from her hands.

"Hertha is having some mead in the small meeting room," said Gita.

Brenna glanced in her direction. "And you are telling me this, why?"

Gita raised her eyebrows in response.

Grunting, she rinsed her hands in the water before starting on her face and neck.

"I'll bring another tankard and fill the pitcher," said Gita before leaving the room.

Brenna scrubbed harder, then splashed water over her face. Gita was right, she could not put this off any longer. They were going to war and she needed to know exactly how her mother felt about her secret being revealed.

Reaching for a dry linen, she patted her face and neck dry. Her mother would want to know the same thing of her. Bile rose in her throat. For that, she had no answer.

Brenna pulled her shoulders back. She was the Jarl of Birca and that was who would be speaking with Hertha. Before she could change her mind, she headed for the meeting room.

Her mother sat at the table in the same seat she'd occupied last night. Her back was straight but her eyes looked weary. A tankard was placed in front of her. In the centre of the table was a second cup and a pitcher of mead.

"Hello, Mother."

She poured herself some mead and took a seat.

Hertha's smile was small and tired. "Brenna, I am happy you are here."

"You've heard King Aric's plan to find more allies to fight against Gorm?" This was the only conversation she wanted to have.

Her mother sighed. "Ja, Ragnar told me."

"You have said many times that you do not want the people of Gyldarhagi to suffer any more." Brenna twisted the cup between her hands. "But they do suffer. Gorm is not a ruler for all the people. He cares only for his warriors that can bring him riches. Many are hungry and sick."

Brenna stiffened as her mother slid her hand over her own.

"It is not right that the people of Gyldarhagi struggle while Gorm's wealth grows as a result of his raids in the west." Brenna kept speaking, not willing to let the discussion take a more personal turn.

"Nei, it is not," said Hertha gently. "But it is not my fight."

"People will fight in your name."

"Mayhap. It matters not what I want." Hertha's smile tightened. "The King has given his command."

Brenna slipped her hand free, grasping her cup. She took a long draft of the honeyed liquid, dreading the conversation she knew her mother wanted to have with her.

"Keeping the truth from you was never meant to cause you pain."

She placed the cup back on the table. She wanted to get

up and leave, but she willed herself to stay. As much as she hated knowing that Gorm was her father, she needed to understand her parents' motivation in keeping it from her.

"All I ever wanted - all Ragnar and I ever wanted, was to keep you safe."

Heat crept up her neck while tears pricked the back of her eyes. "Why did you come here?"

Hertha shafted in her seat. "What?"

"Why were you on the drakkar?"

Her mother nodded her understanding. "When I heard Gorm was in Birca, I had to come. Call it a mother's instinct, but I needed to see with my own eyes that you were safe."

A tear broke free and ran down Brenna's cheek, momentarily breaking her resolve to remain the Jarl, and not her mother's child.

"And now I've managed to make everything so much worse." Hertha wrung her hands on the table.

Brenna shook her head, hastily palming the tears from her face. "Gorm cannot be allowed to sit on the throne of Gyldarhagi. Your presence has changed everything. Finally, he will be defeated."

"I hope so, Daughter."

I will kill him. For the people of Gyldarhagi... and for you, Mother.

19

*V*ali had not had an opportunity to speak with Brenna this morning. She left the great hall very quickly; he was certain she was avoiding her mother, her father and almost definitely him. He knew she would be throwing herself into some task, as was her way. She dealt with the emotional through physical distraction - training, preparing for the battle, or whatever she could do so as not to feel helpless and idle. That suited him. Today, he had his own task to see too.

When Ivar left the great hall, Vali followed.

His suspicions of the man had not been enough for Brenna to even consider that he may be the source of her challenges in Birca. Vali had paid a farmer handsomely for his oldest hooded cloak, a heavy fabric that had been patched many times over. Now, with it covering his own clothes, he blended into the crowd with ease.

Ivar spent the rest of the morning and early afternoon with Eric and Snorri, spreading word of the impending attack and preparing the army for battle. In plain sight of anyone and everyone. Vali chose an ale house, favoured by the servants, from which he could observe.

No matter, he thought, *I can be patient.*

"If you're going to sit here, you need to buy a drink," said a servant woman.

He glanced up into narrowed eyes. He pushed a coin across the table.

The coin disappeared as ale sloshed into a tankard.

At that moment, something caught Ivar's eye. Vali followed his stare and saw the wanderer who'd brought news of Gorm this morning making his way to the field where the horses were kept. He watched as Ivar excused himself and went after the wanderer.

At last! Vali stood, adrenaline coursing through his body. He would need to skirt around the training ground if he wanted to remain unnoticed. He made haste, not wanting to lose Ivar from his sight for too long.

He found Ivar and the wanderer outside the hut where Elof kept the tack and saddles. The men were deep in conversation. Vali cut behind Elof's cottage in order to watch without being seen.

Ivar reached across and clapped his hand on the other man's shoulder, speaking rapidly. Vali grunted, he could not make out the words. The wanderer nodded. Ivar took a small leather pouch from his belt and handed it over.

Níðingr!

The wanderer measured its weight in his hand before tying it to his own belt.

Vali pulled his head back behind the cottage as Ivar glanced in his direction. When he looked again, Ivar was walking away and the wanderer was untying a horse tethered to the fence, saddled and ready. He mounted and pointed the horse west, in the direction one would ride if you were headed towards Fornsigtuna, or Gyldarhagi.

Thor's blood, Vali cursed again. There were many reasons Ivar could be giving the man coins, but Vali was sure his intentions were not honourable. Still, he had no proof of Ivar's betrayal and Brenna would not hear any more of his suspicions.

Movement behind the hut caught his eye. Elof's son, Leif stepped out from the shadows. A flicker of hope stirred.

Vali left his hiding place, striding towards the boy. "Leif!"

Leif looked startled, his eyes darting to the cottage where undoubtedly, he hoped someone would come to his rescue.

"It is Vali Hrolfsson," he said, pulling the hood back from his head.

Leif nodded in recognition, but his face remained pensive. "Well met, Vali."

"I saw Ivar of Bulandshofoi speaking with a man who claimed to be a wanderer."

The boy nodded again.

"Leif, I will be honest with you."Vali drew himself up, speaking to the boy as he would another man. "I do not trust these men. But I could not get close enough to hear what they spoke of."

He watched as Leif processed what he was saying, some of the strain leaving his features. "I heard them talking."

"Ja? That is good." The flicker of hope roared into being. "Can you tell me what was said?"

Leif looked around nervously. "I would speak with my father first."

Vali would not be put off. "What you heard; was it talk of treason?"

The boy swallowed hard. He was right to be mindful of

repeating a traitor's tale. If he was not believed, he could find himself facing the axe.

"Leif? Is everything alright?"

Vali turned to see Elof heading towards them from across the field. Despite the loss of his arm and eye, Elof was still an imposing man and well-respected by all. He would get his son to talk.

"Look, it is your father. We can discuss this together, ja?"

"Is that Vali Hrolfsson? Well met, Styrimaor. Are you in need of a horse?"

"Well met, Elof. It is not a horse I am in need of today."

"Oh?" Elof turned his good eye closer to look at Vali.

Vali explained he had been following Ivar and the wanderer and believed Leif had overheard talk of treason.

Elof faced his son. "If you know something that places our Jarl in danger, you must share it now." His voice was firm but gentle.

The boy's shoulders relaxed. Vali knew Elof would let no harm befall his son while he drew breath.

"Ivar of Bulandshofoi thanked the wanderer for keeping his word," began Leif.

Vali's heart beat sped up. "Did he say exactly what he had done?"

"Ja, he told Jarl Brenna and King Aric that the people of Gyldarhagi were suffering under Gorm's rule."

It would not be enough to convince Brenna of wrongdoing, he knew.

"What more was said?" He tried to keep the need out of his voice, not wanting to influence the boy or his father.

"Ivar told the wanderer to ride directly to Gyldarhagi. He was to warn Gorm that King Aric is bringing together a large army of allies loyal to the murdered king and his family."

Vali clenched his fists. He was right!

Leif continued. "Ivar said to tell Gorm that Princess Ingrid lives, and that he has an heir."

"Níðingr," hissed Vali. He knew Ivar was a snake, but this was much worse than he'd feared. Did the man really have no fealty to Brenna after so many months by her side?

"We must tell the Jarl and the King." Elof drew himself up to his full height

"Nei," Vali placed his hand on Elof's shoulder. "Let me tell Jarl Brenna." *Not that she'll want to* hear *it from me either.*

"What of the King?" asked Elof.

Vali looked to the old warrior. "Elof, you have fought in many battles and one day you will feast in the golden hall of Valhalla. But you must know that Aric is not one to fight a battle he is not sure he will win."

Elof nodded slowly. "Ja, you are right, Vali. Jarl Brenna should hear of this and decide what is the best course of action."

"Thank you, Elof." He turned to the boy. "Thank you, Leif."

He left in search of Brenna. This time, she had to believe him!

Losing the cloak, Vali moved through the marketplace and onto the great hall. Inside was a hive of activity, but there was no sign of Brenna. Catching Gita's eye, he motioned for her to meet him at the door.

"What is it, Vali?"

"Have you seen Brenna? I must speak with her."

"She went to the docks to inspect the boats. They sail for Fornsigtuna at dawn."

"Thank you."

Gita stopped him with a hand on his forearm. "Is everything alright?"

"No, Gita, it's not."

Every moment counted. He must get to Brenna. With a tight smile, he took his leave.

AT THE DOCKS, Brenna was deep in conversation with Eric. Her drakkars had been kept in excellent condition, despite their lack of use over the summer. Still, sails were inspected, oars checked for cracks and ropes were unfurled and carefully rolled back.

As he approached, Eric inclined his head to Brenna and started back towards the town.

"Vali," he called. "Just the man I was looking for. You will sail with the Jarl to Fornsigtuna?"

"We sail at dawn?" Vali kept his face neutral. He may have been the styrimaor of his own ship, but Eric, along with Snorri, was responsible for commanding Brenna's army.

"Ja."

The two men paused as they came face to face. Vali glanced towards Brenna.

"I will sail with the Jarl."

Eric nodded. "Good. That leaves Snorri and I to command the second boat. I'll not keep you." Eric clapped him on the shoulder and continued on his way.

Brenna had boarded one of the boats and was helping to store the oars. Birca's war boats held about sixty men on each, with thirteen oar ports on either side. They were much smaller than Aric's drakkars, which could hold one hundred warriors.

Vali crouched down on the dock next to her. Her long blonde hair had been hastily braided into one plait down her back. She wore trousers and tunic, looking like any other sailor preparing for a voyage.

"Brenna?"

She squinted up at him. "Vali, did Eric find you?"

Some things will never change, thought Vali. *Always so focused on the practical.*

"He did. But it is you I must speak with now."

She placed the final oar in position. Rising, Vali offered her his hand and helped her from the vessel.

"I don't have much time. I must oversee the packing at the great hall and then prepare for the funeral rites this evening." She began moving along the dock.

"Funeral rites?"

"For the warriors who died in the longhouse fire."

"Of course." He reached for her to slow her progress. "Brenna. I have news that you will not like hearing."

She closed her eyes for a moment, rubbing her hand across her forehead. "What more could there be."

"It is Ivar-"

"No! Vali, why can you not let this go?" Her eyes were alight with anger.

"Please, listen to me." He tried to keep his own frustration at bay. "You said I had no proof of Ivar's disloyalty, so today, I followed him."

"That's what you have been doing all day?" she interrupted. Her arm swung wildly out to her side. "The whole town has been working in the defence of Birca and you have been playing the spy!"

He ignored her tone, and the looks from those around them readying the boats and continued. "He met with the wanderer who came to town this morning. He thanked the man for keeping his word and telling you the people of Gyldarhagi suffer-"

"This is your proof?" Her face was incredulous.

"Listen!" he hissed. "He paid this man and sent him to warn Gorm of the plan to attack him."

Brenna pursed her lips. "You heard him say this?"

He took a deep breath. "Nei."

"Nei?"

"I was not close enough. Elof's son, Leif was there. He heard everything."

She shook her head, her frown fading "Leif wanted to come and fight this battle and I told him nei. I can well imagine he might be feeling slighted."

"That is not the case, let me assure you. Elof was there-"

"Elof heard this exchange?"

If she would just stop interrupting him.

"Nei, he was not." He held up his hand before she could speak again. "You cannot ignore this, Brenna. Gorm knows we are coming."

She stared at him, the challenge still in her eyes.

"Ivar also told the wanderer to tell Gorm that his eyes did not deceive him; Princess Ingrid lives." He lowered his voice. "And that he has an heir."

Brenna's face remained neutral but the distant stirring of a storm flashed behind her eyes. "You're asking me to trust the word of a boy no more than thirteen summers? A boy I just told could not come to battle with me."

"You can trust what I saw with my own eyes." He stepped closer. "Elof and I spoke with Leif and we both believe he speaks the truth."

He reached for her, placing his hands on each of her arms. "You can rely on their discretion. They all agreed that you should decide what to make of this information."

"Good." She shrugged his hands from her arms and

stepped back from him. "I will say this for the final time. I trust Ivar."

"By the gods, Brenna-"

Her eyes narrowed into a cold, hard stare. "You saw what you wanted to see, Vali. And you have corrupted Leif into believing he heard what you want to believe."

Red, hot anger tore through his veins. She had dismissed him without even considering the possibility that he spoke the truth! No more! He would take no more of her mistrust. He needed to be gone from here, before he took the matter into his own hands.

"If you cannot trust me, I will not stay," he said through gritted teeth.

"So, I must choose between you and Ivar?" She raised her eyebrows, mocking him.

"You already have." He walked away without looking back.

20

*B*renna watched as Vali marched away, her body trembling with rage. How dare he use the secret of her parentage to try and sway her! It was enough that Aric had spread the word of Ingrid's existence, but to claim that Ivar would expose her in this way? And to use Leif as his proof...It was if Loki himself had taken the form of Vali, so great was this deceit.

She clenched her fists and took a deep breath, calling on the wisdom of Frigga to guide her. Of all the goddesses, Frigga knew too well the pain of having her trust betrayed by Loki. Yet she remained the Queen of Asgard. So too, would Brenna fulfil her role as Jarl and protector of her people. Pulling back her shoulder and raising her chin, she let go of Vali's insinuations. She had work to do.

The busyness of preparing for war was evident everywhere she looked. Her town was crowded thanks to Aric's army. Many of his warriors were making their way to the horses. They would leave before the sunset to return overland to Fornsigtuna.

In the great hall, the servants were piling provisions into

sacks for warriors. Bread, cheese and dried meats would keep the hunger at bay as they travelled to Fornsigtuna, and then on to Gyldarhagi.

"Jarl Brenna," called King Aric from the dais on which he sat on her chair. "There you are."

She approached, mindful of keeping a neutral facade even though she bristled at the King sitting in her place while she had been out working with her people.

Below Aric, on the floor stood Ragnar and Hertha. Her father turned, his face thunderous. Hertha's complexion was pale and drawn. What was happening now?

"King Aric," she said as she came to stand beside her father.

"Brenna," he began. "I have decided to return to Fornsigtuna by sea. Ragnar will lead the men overland."

She saw no issue with that. What had gotten her father so angry?

"And Princess Ingrid will sail with me."

Brenna's stomach dropped and she swore she saw lightning flash in Ragnar's eyes.

"Again Sire, I would feel more comfortable if *Hertha* travelled with me."

"She will be perfectly safe with me, Ragnar. You are my chief huscarl, you must lead the men home."

Out of the corner of her eye, Brenna saw her mother slip her hand into Ragnar's. It seemed the King was in no mood to grant his closest friend any favours.

"Jarl Brenna," Aric interrupted her thoughts. "As Vali has decided to ride out for Fornsigtuna ahead of the army, I have entrusted him with speaking to Queen Ylva of our plans."

Vali was actually leaving. Her surprise must have shown.

"You were not aware of Vali's plans?" asked Aric. "No

matter, he left only moments ago if you wish to go after him."

An ache settled around her heart. He did not even say goodbye to her.

"Ragnar, the men are assembling." Aric gave him a pointed look.

Ragnar gave a slight bow. "I will say goodbye to my family." He looked to Brenna and she nodded that she would follow. She needed to know how Hertha felt about travelling with Aric, and not her husband.

At the entrance to the private quarters, she hesitated when Ivar called her name. She turned to face him.

"Jarl, I heard the exchange between Ragnar and the King."

She waited for him to continue.

"With your permission, I will travel with the King and watch over your mother. Mayhap that will give Ragnar some peace of mind?"

Brenna squeezed his arm. "Thank you, Ivar. You are right, it will ease my father's mind some to know you are there."

Ivar returned her smile and left.

Vali was a fool to try and dissuade her of Ivar's loyalty. And now he had run away. At least it was one less distraction for her to deal with. Their allies were gathering and would meet in Fornsigtuna over the next few days. Finally, she would have the chance to rip the throne of Gyldarhagi away from the Usurper and right the wrongs of the past.

21

*B*renna laid a soothing hand on the neck of her horse as they halted their advance. The battle horns echoed across the mountain top. They were still an hour's march to Gyldarhagi, but scouts had brought word that Gorm's army was moving out to meet them. From this position, they would have the initial advantage of higher ground.

Six Jarls had answered Aric's call, the combined forces numbering some six hundred warriors. Jarl Tollak of Ostergotland and Jarl Fritjof of Vastergotland from the south had brought smaller forces. Their territories were rich farming lands and their harvests required many hands. Jarl Bjorn of Skane, a neighbour further south, had also answered the call.

Asketill of Uppsala and his men had met up with Ragnar as he and the King's army returned to Fornsigtuna. From the north, Jarl Ingolf of Jamtland and Jarl Gleb of Harjedalen had arrived only the day before. Their skill on the battlefield was retold in many ale houses and halls across the land. Together, the eight armies were an impressive force. Hopefully impressive enough to make quick work of Gorm and his army.

Gorm, sitting astride a horse, and his men lined up in the valley below; he looked to have close to four hundred warriors. Brenna could not see any other flags indicating Gorm had his own allies. If Gorm could call his jarls to battle and add a further two hundred warriors waiting for him, it was little wonder no one had attacked the war lord before now.

Aric sent word for the archers to take aim. The order echoed from one army to the next. Gorm's men formed a shield wall. Brenna spied Gorm's horse being led away to the forest of trees behind them, as they readied for battle.

"Hear me Tyr, Odin and Thor before this fight," she whispered. "Grant me your courage, wisdom and strength to smite this Usurper."

She dismounted from her horse, giving the reins to a servant to lead him to safety. Unclasping her shield from her back, Brenna slid it onto her arm. She took her axe from her belt. Anticipation coursed through her veins.

"Loose!" Came the call to release the arrows. The whistle of two hundred arrows filled the air, followed by the thunk against shields and the cry of wood penetrating flesh.

"Nock!"

The archers reloaded.

"Loose!"

Brenna turned to face her warriors. "Today we take vengeance on Gorm. Vengeance for his attack on Birca! Vengeance for his attack on Gyldarhagi!"

Her army cheered at her words.

"We fight for our ancestors!"

The roar grew louder.

"We fight for the All-father!"

Weapons banged on shields, adding to the deafening sound. Across the mountain, battle cries roared loud enough to be heard in Asgard.

Brenna slammed her axe against her shield, adding her own howl to the mix. She would fight for her people, for Hertha and the life that was stolen from her, for her true father Ragnar and his strength. She screamed to block the absence of Vali from her mind. Today, she would have her vengeance.

"Nock!"

As the archers took aim, Brenna and the rest of the warriors descended in a tidal wave of fury.

"Loose!"

Arrows flew overhead, reaching their destination moments before the warriors. The shield wall immediately gave way, intending to trap a section of the attacking force inside. Their armies were ready for this, rushing as many of their own people into the centre of Gorm's men as possible. Most of the archers discarded their bows and were on their way to join the battle below. It was Gorm who would be surrounded from the inside and the exterior.

Bodies were jammed tightly and Brenna used her small form to her advantage, building momentum to swing her axe as she pivoted on the spot. She ducked low, beneath the shields, to slice at the legs of her enemy. When they fell, she spun up and swung hard at their heads, dodging the blades aimed at her.

She opened the vein of one Viking, his blood spraying the air and her face, reminding her of the sacrifices they made to the gods before they began this battle.

"For Odin!" she roared.

The heavy blow of a shield to her side knocked her forward, sending her off-balance. She turned and raised her own shield, blocking an axe as it plummeted towards her head. The Viking heaved his shield at her again, sending her sprawling on her backside into the ground. Rage and adrenaline fired through her.

She rolled to the left as the axe came for her again. Springing to her feet, she finally got a look at her attacker. He was a giant of a man, with a long red beard. His head was shaved bald and he wore no body armour. His eyes were glazed and the sneer on his lips showed he believed this kill was imminent.

You underestimate me, fifl.

She knew she had the advantage if she was fast enough to get beneath the length of his reach. Pushing her axe into her belt, she removed her dagger. She cracked her neck from side to side then motioned for the Viking to attack. He snorted and swung his axe over his head. At the point it started to arc downwards, Brenna ran towards his exposed torso. She plunged the dagger into his side, aiming between the fourth and fifth ribs.

He growled as she pulled the knife free, then smashed his head hard against her. It glanced off her cheekbone and opened the flesh. Her vision blurred and her skull rang as if Thor beat his anvil inside of it. Either she'd missed her mark or she was fighting a monster with no heart. On instinct, she raised her shield, managing to block another swinging axe. She squeezed her eyes shut, then opened them, hoping to see clearly. The axe swung again; she blocked it. This monster would not get the better of her.

The ringing in her head eased a little, and the world came back into focus. Replacing her knife, she ducked another blow and reached for her sword. Blood dripped from the Viking's mouth. Mayhap she'd found her mark after all. He dropped his shield and wrapped both hands around his axe, raising it above his head. The volume of his roar rattled her brain. She lunged forward with her sword, driving it through his heart.

He did not fall. His eyes were molten with rage. Was this Loki in disguise, playing with her? Brenna smashed her shield up under his chin, jerking her sword free. Still, he did not go down.

By Thor's blood, how is this possible?

His axe swung at her again, slicing through her sleeve, beneath the mail. The blade did not find bone, but her blood ran freely down her arm. She would need to stem the flow before it stole too much of her strength.

The Viking was weakening, yet he kept coming at her. She gritted her teeth and took aim at his arms, needing to find a way to stop his axe. Before she could strike, a spear pierced the Viking through the back of his neck. In slow motion, he fell to his knees, his axe dropping to his side. Blood covered his body like a dark red cloak. As the light faded from his eyes, he fell forward onto the ground.

Relief flooded her senses. Never had she faced an opponent she could not slay. Behind the corpse stood Ivar. He nodded before turning to ward off a blow from another warrior.

She drew in a ragged breath. She had been right to trust Ivar. She lived to fight again because of his loyalty.

Gorm's army was outnumbered in warriors only. They were seasoned fighters and most had the berserker spirit within them. They would gladly fight until death.

Ivar appeared at her side. "Jarl, you are wounded?"

She examined the cut on her arm; blood was dripping onto the ground. "I just need to tie it off and it will be fine."

"We can do that once we get to the forest." He started to move away from the battlefield.

She frowned. "What are you talking about?"

Turning back, he explained. "I came to find you. Gorm left the battle as soon as it began."

"What?" *Why would he run from a fight?*

"He has something planned, I'm sure of it."

Another warrior surged towards them. Ivar's sword clashed with his attackers. "Go Jarl, I'll meet you at the trees."

Brenna stumbled out of the way. She gathered her wits and fought her way to the back of the battle ground. As she pulled her sword free from the neck of an enemy warrior, she scanned the tree line, common sense telling her to look for signs of a trap. Seeing no movement or glint of metal against the sun, she made for the forest.

Dappled shadows welcomed her. She appeared to be quite alone.

Her arm had begun to throb and her sleeve was dark with blood. She reached beneath the leather corset and using her dagger, cut the bottom of her linen tunic into a long strip. Placing one end in her mouth, she tied a bandage around the wound, stemming the blood flow.

The battle had been vicious. She felt Gorm's men would not concede, preferring to fight until they were victorious or every last one of them lay dead. Still, the King's allies were holding up well. Surely, they would succeed.

They had to.

Footfall interrupted her thoughts. She slipped the dagger back in her belt and retrieved her axe. The tree she'd been leaning on was wide enough to provide cover. Her muscles tensed as she waited to see if friend or foe would be revealed.

"Ivar," she exhaled the breath she'd been holding, leaning back against the tree to rest for a moment more.

Blood stained his red hair and beard darker. "Jarl, are you well?"

"Ja, Ivar." She needed to know why she was here and not fighting with her army. "Are you sure you saw Gorm leave from here?"

"Ja, I am sure. He walked his horse away from the attack."

Brenna remembered seeing the horse being led away. She had not considered it was Gorm holding the reins. "Why would he not stay and fight?"

"I don't know, but he must have something planned. He headed back in the direction of Gyldarhagi."

What to do? It did not sit well to leave while the battle still raged. But if Gorm was planning something more, she wanted to find him and put a stop to it.

Standing up, she slipped the axe back into her belt. "We'll go to Gyldarhagi."

_____

22

*V*ali regretted his self-control in not killing Ivar on the battlefield the moment he watched him follow Brenna into the forest. To be honest, he'd regretted it when Ivar killed that Viking. It appeared the giant of a man had the upper hand over Brenna, but he'd never doubted Brenna's ability to overcome her enemy.

Except in the case of Ivar.

Vali surveyed the battle, easily finding Ragnar now the fighting had spread out. The huscarl had lost naught of his strength and cunning as a warrior, sending over a dozen men to Valhalla since the fight began.

Removing the cloak he wore to disguise his presence as he waited and watched for Ivar to make his move, Vali waded into the melee, striking out against those who sought to engage him. Gorm's men were ruthless, and not so easy to dispatch. Keeping his shield strapped to his back, Vali hacked and swung his sword and axe without any patience for the art of warfare. He must get to Ragnar.

A shadow came from behind, stopping Vali in his tracks. He turned to find a man as tall and broad as Thor himself staring him down with the decree of death in his eyes. The beast roared, raising his double-headed axe above his head as he rushed at him.

Vali lunged forward, crossing his weapons above his own head to ward off the blow. For an instant, the beast was close enough for Vali to see the haze of bloodlust set deep within him.

Berserker.

Keeping his axe raised, Vali pivoted and brought his sword across the belly of the beast. Blood fell like a veil from the cut, but it did not slow him. The axe swung low towards Vali's head. He pulled back, the blade close enough for him to see traces of blood and flesh. The axe came again. He should not have withdrawn. Vali blocked as best he could, needing a split second reprieve in which to regain his footing.

Finally, the moment came and he charged closer, thrusting his sword into the wound on the beast's belly. The Viking snarled and Vali hacked with his axe, connecting with flesh and bone. The roar was deafening; the mangled arm hanging uselessly at his side.

Any other man would be dead, but the beast was still on his feet, weapon in hand, still looking for Vali's blood. The axe chopped through the air, back and forth, giving Vali no chance to attack. The beast fought with the spirit of Tyr within, but he could not prevail. Vali knew today was not his day to perish.

Summoning the strength of all his ancestors, Vali unleashed his battle cry. He caught the beast's axe as it swung at him again with his own axe, then brought his sword down upon his arm. Blood sprayed through the air, covering Vali's face and torso. With one almighty pivot into the air, he smashed his axe into the neck of the beast.

The Viking stood his ground, stretching his lips into a bloody grin. "Valhalla." He fell.

Vali released a ragged breath.

"Ragnar!" he bellowed, turning in a close circle. He'd lost so much time.

"Vali!"

The two men made their way to one another across bloodied mud strewn with dead and broken warriors. Metal continued to crash amidst the primal language of battle.

"Where have you been?" asked Ragnar.

"I'll explain. But you must come with me. Ivar and Brenna headed towards the forest." He spoke rapidly. "Towards Gyldarhagi."

"Why?"

"I do not know, but Ivar is not what he seems."

Ragnar eyed the younger man.

"Ragnar?" Desperation crept into his tone. He prayed to the gods that Ragnar did not think him merely jealous of Ivar. "Do you see Gorm anywhere on the battlefield?"

The huscarl's eyes darted all around, realisation draining the colour from his face.

"Alright," he nodded.

They headed towards the trees, making short work of any attacks between them.

As they reached the forest, the cacophony of battle barely fading behind them, Ragnar spoke again. "Does Brenna know you are here?"

"Nei, she will not listen to anything against Ivar. It blinds her from the truth." Vali did not slow his step, forging his way deeper into the forest.

"Which is?"

Vali repeated what he had witnessed between Ivar and the wanderer.

"You believe Leif?" Ragnar kept pace beside him.

"I do. I came to Fornsigtuna ahead of Brenna so I could watch Ivar."

The forest was strangely quiet after the chaos of the battlefield. They lowered their voices.

Vali moved swiftly, staying alert for any signs of danger. "Ivar has clearly bewitched the King as well."

"What do you mean?" asked Ragnar.

The forest grew darker as the trees shielded the sun from penetrating.

"Why else would Aric entrust him with getting Hertha to safety?"

Ragnar halted. "What are you talking about?"

Vali turned back to face him. "I saw Ivar and a small guard of huscarl escorting Hertha to a boat."

Alarm registered on Ragnar's face. "Hertha was to wait with Queen Ylva and the gothi at the temple," he whispered.

Fear threatened to strangle all the oxygen from Vali's lungs. The huscarl's loyalty was sworn in blood. "But the huscarl-"

"Would not betray their King."

Imposters!

"If Gorm has Hertha and Brenna, we will need more men. You have been to Gyldarhagi," said Vali, making the decision with his head and not his heart. "I will go back and bring more warriors."

Ragnar nodded. "May the gods go with you."

"And you."

As the forest gave way to a clearing, Brenna was stunned by what she saw across the field. Gyldarhagi was surrounded by a large circular wall, with equally spaced ramparts, reinforced with a barricade of wooden stakes. The town appeared impenetrable. It must be a trap?

"How can we gain access?" She placed her hand on Ivar's arm to stop his progress. "They will see us coming and of course there will be guards stationed at the gate."

"It looks that way, I know," he said. "But I have been inside the fortress, many years ago. The outer wall was still being built."

"Does it encircle the entire town?" She watched for movement along the wooden ramparts, but the fortress appeared strangely quiet. Almost deserted.

"I believe that was the plan. I think there is also another wall inside of that one, made of earth and timber. There should be four gates in total, including the one that leads to the docks."

Brenna shook her head. "I have never seen such a thing."

Ivar inclined his head closer to hers. "It is said Gorm studied the fortresses and defences of the places he raided, then created his own fortress with none of the weaknesses he'd found in others."

She could not deny the fortress of Gyldarhagi was impressive, even as her eyes scanned the perimeter for weaknesses "How do we get inside?"

"By the size of the army Gorm took to the battlefield, I would say there are only a few warriors left to defend the town," said Ivar. "Anyone approaching the fortress would react as you and I have."

Brenna nodded. "And by that logic, would try to gain access from another side."

Ivar grinned. "If I were king, I would put my guards at the other entrances."

"I've not seen any sign of guards at this gate." She

sheathed her sword, and slid her shield onto her arm. "Let's run straight for the gate."

"Agreed."

Heimdall, lend me your sight and guard us from attack.

"Ready?"

He raised his axe in agreement.

She took a deep breath and broke into a sprint, holding her shield above her head with her good arm. Ivar kept pace beside her. She strained her ears for the sound of arrows in the air, or a shout or battle horn announcing their presence. Mayhap the beating of her heart blocked any other noise?

Seconds stretched into minutes; she pumped her legs harder, finally reaching the outer wall. They rested for a moment, catching their breath. They appeared to have arrived undetected.

"I don't like this, Ivar." She glanced at him crouched beside her.

"The gods are with us."

She hoped that was true, but her gut warned her this must be a trap. Brenna had never seen a fortress such as this, but Gorm was no fool. There had to be a reason why he'd left the entrance unguarded.

Unsheathing her sword, she jerked her head towards the open gate. Ignoring the ache in her wounded arm, she edged her way forward. All was quiet. Once inside, Brenna checked the ramparts for guards but found them all empty. Her gut tightened. Definitely a trap. Still, she couldn't turn back; she must find Gorm.

Ivar had been correct; another wall stood several faðmr inside. This one was shorter and consisted of timber frames and mud bricks. Again, a gate stood open. Brenna could make out the shape of longhouses and could see smoke spiralling upwards, she guessed from the fire pits inside the structures.

They moved quickly between the two walls, flattening their backs against the second. Brenna glanced around the gate. The road was dug out and continued straight across from this gate to what appeared to be another in the distance. A longhouse lined either side of the road.

"Jarl," whispered Ivar. "We should split up. I will follow the road this way." He nodded his head to the right of the gate.

"Alright," she agreed. It made sense not to stand on top of each other.

Leading with outstretched swords, they crept along the longhouse wall. A muffled sound came from the house behind Ivar. He indicated he would investigate while Brenna continued on.

Where were all the townspeople? From what she could see, Gyldarhagi seemed to be divided into four sections. Surely the people lived inside the walls? She'd seen no sign of life at all.

She glanced behind her. Ivar had disappeared, following the noise they'd heard. Brenna edged along the front of the long house. It was built in a group of four, with a smaller hut in the middle. All of the doors were closed; linens hung against the windows. Nothing stirred.

Her heart beat against her ribcage, as though trying to break free. She did not like this. Behind Gyldarhagi was a great mountain range. Mayhap the people hid there, as they did in Birca? But where were the guards?

She came to another road that crossed the one she followed. It too, had a gate at either end. She noted they were firmly closed, as was the one she walked towards. Movement caught her eye. Brenna sprang back against the wall of the longhouse. There were guards watching these gates. She watched each gate in turn. A single warrior watched outward from atop the ramparts. A seagull called out to her left. This gate led to the fjord.

Taking a deep breath, she slipped across the road and into the shadow of the longhouse. Only two longhouses sat adjacent to the roads. The middle was open space. Brenna gave a small gasp as she saw the great hall that loomed above it all.

Two elaborately carved beams stood at the entrance of the hall, the pitched roof reaching high into the sky over a balcony. She guessed the living quarters were upstairs, leaving the bottom level as a massive mead hall. King Aric and Queen Ylva's hall was similarly constructed in Fornsigtuna. While her grandparents had been King and Queen of Gyldarhagi, she'd never thought of Gorm as a King. His hall - nei, her ancestors' hall - radiated power.

"So glad you could join us, Daughter!"

The booming voice drew her eyes upwards, to the balcony once more. Staring down at her, was Gorm. Beside him, holding her tight with his hand fisted into her hair, stood Hertha.

23

"*M*other!"

Panic threatened to shut down her senses. How had Gorm found Hertha? She was supposed to be safe with Queen Ylva in Fornsigtuna.

"Nei, run Brenna-"

Gorm slapped Hertha across her face, then dragged her from Brenna's sight.

She saw nothing but red. Instinct took over. Brenna ran to the double doors, heaving them open. The great hall was empty of people. Long tables and benches ran the length of the room, shields and carvings adorned the walls, and furs and skins lay across the massive dais at the very end, where a huge carved chair covered with furs sat in the middle. Brenna guessed the stairwell leading to the private quarters was somewhere behind the throne.

As she made her way through the great hall, a wind whispered past her, leaving an echo of familiarity. She slowed her steps, without meaning to. The haze of red shimmered behind her eyes, then fell away, wrapping her fury in a finely spun linen resonating in calm and patience that felt... old.

She'd come to a complete stop. Brenna found the urgent need to get to her mother had been caught up on the breeze that flowed past her, floating just out of her reach.

"They are here..."

Brenna spun around. There was no one there. Yet, she felt she was not alone.

"They are watching you..."

She wanted to speak but she had no words.

"... You will fulfil the destiny of your ancestors. You will heal the scars that run deep in their veins."

A shiver ran down her spine.

"My destiny..." she whispered, *"is determined by my actions."*

"The blood of your ancestors runs through you...

"...and the strength of the gods are with you...

"It has been fated."

The wind fluttered towards the throne, then all was still. She knew what she had to do.

Brenna slowly faced the carved chair on the dais. It was not the throne of her ancestors, and she would never sit upon a false king's throne.

"By Odin's eye, no one will sit on this throne again."

She found the staircase behind a heavy curtain, dividing the great hall from the kitchen and servant's quarters. The stairs led to the attic. A long fire pit ran down the centre of the floor, giving light and warmth to each of the narrow alcoves on either side. A larger space at the end of the room was clearly the bedchamber of Gorm.

He stood in the middle of the space, holding her mother by the neck. An ugly red welt covered the left side of her face. Brenna swallowed the anger that rose inside her.

"You did not run." Gorm gave her an admiring grin.

She shook her head. It would take a different kind of strength to defeat this monster and free her mother.

"Are you hoping Aric rides to your rescue again?"

"Nei," she said.

Removing the shield from her back, she laid it on the ground and began walking towards him.

"I did not know who you were," she said quietly. "When you landed on my shores."

She removed the axe from her belt and let it drop to the floor. "It was a secret that was kept from me my whole life."

Gorm watched her through narrowed eyes.

"It's true," whispered Hertha.

Brenna unsheathed her sword, and carried it to where Gorm and her mother stood.

"And now the truth has been revealed to us both," Gorm smirked. "What has that changed for you?"

She knelt and laid her sword at his feet, mindful to keep her eyes on his. "It changes everything, Father."

Hertha hissed, but said nothing.

Gorm's features had not softened any. "Why should I believe you?"

She rose to her feet. "You do not know me, but you should recognise my ambition."

He tilted his head.

"It has always been my desire to rule. And ja, I am the Jarl of Birca - a position I claimed for myself." She continued to look him in the eye. "I did not know Sigurd the Black was my brother, but it makes no difference. He was weak, paying others to do his bidding while he watched on."

The corner of his mouth lifted. "You are a mighty shield maiden."

She inclined her head in acknowledgment.

"And now you want the crown of Gyldarhagi?" There was a challenge in his voice.

"It is my fate to rule this land."

"Your fate?"

She took a step closer. "Did you not make it so, Father, when you bedded my mother and produced a true heir to the throne?"

He raised an eyebrow. "And what of Ragnar Eriksson?"

"He taught me how to fight," she forced a calculating smile on her face. "But he intended me to follow, when I was born to rule."

Gorm chuckled, the sound turning her stomach sour.

Brenna looked at Hertha, praying her voice would not betray her words. "Mother, would you not stay here in Gyldarhagi, your rightful home, if I choose to stay?"

"What are you saying, Brenna?" Tears filled Hertha's eyes and her voice was choked.

"This is my destiny; it could be yours too."

Please understand *what I am saying!*

There was a flicker of recognition in her mother's eyes. "I will never leave you again, Brenna."

Brenna smiled, and turned her gaze back to Gorm. "Is this not what you wanted, Father?"

He looked from Brenna to Hertha, his eyes lingering on her mother. Slowly, he released his grip on her neck. Hertha stood her ground, straightening her shoulders and lifting her chin.

"My Queen," he whispered.

"And you are now the Princess of Gyldarhagi, Brenna," she said.

"I am sure this is what the ancestors have wished for me." Brenna inclined her head to her mother.

"Father," she took another step closer. "We must discuss

the battle that rages beyond the forest. Most of those warriors are sworn to you and I. The allies of King Aric have come in the name of Ingrid."

Gorm studied her for a moment. "I will send a man known to both sides to order a parley. I want Aric's crown."

"I-

Brenna stopped short as Ivar emerged from behind her. His smile was one of condescension. The fury that rose within her was tempered by her guilt. Vali had been right all along.

"Princess," he greeted her before turning to her mother. "Queen Ingrid."

Hertha stared at him with a look of utter hatred.

"Ivar," said Gorm. "Find Jarl Halfdan and go to Aric and tell him I wish to negotiate. Halfdan knows what to do."

"Ja, King Gorm." Ivar gave a small bow and turned on his heel, throwing Brenna a last look of conceit.

Brenna clenched her fists behind her back. *Ignore him, Ivar does not matter.*

"What is your plan, Father?"

"I will take Aric as my prisoner. Once Ingrid and I have wed, and you have both been declared Queen and Princess of this land, we will travel to Fornsigtuna and claim Aric's territories for our own."

His intentions were exactly as she had thought. "And King Aric?"

"Will be executed once we claim his throne, along with his wife and child."

Brenna disguised the disgust that washed over her by bowing her head.

"How will you ensure the loyalty of Aric's men?"

"Halfdan will invite them all to the fortress for the negotiations. "They will have no choice, once they are trapped inside these walls."

She reached forward and placed her hand on Gorm's forearm. "I wish to learn the secrets of this fortress."

He smiled down at her. "I will teach you, Daughter."

"That won't be necessary." She returned his smile.

For a split second, Gorm looked puzzled.

With her free hand, Brenna withdrew her dagger, jamming it between the fourth and fifth ribs of the man who'd fathered her. This time, she found her mark.

"I will figure it out myself."

He placed his hand on hers as he fell to his knees.

"Daughter, hand me my axe and let me die a warrior." Blood sputtered as he spoke.

"This axe?"

Brenna's smile was genuine, recognising Ragnar's voice behind her. She pulled her hand free of Gorm's grasp, along with her knife. She and Hertha stepped well back from the dying warlord. Ragnar strode forward, raising the axe above his head.

Gorm's grin was bloody. As he opened his mouth to speak, Ragnar swung the axe, bringing it down on his enemy. Gorm's head rolled across the floor, coming to a stop at Hertha's feet. A fitting end, Brenna thought.

24

*V*ali found Eric and Snorri, knowing Aric would put more weight on their word. Once the hersirs understood what they must do, Vali headed back towards Gyldarhagi. He could not wait for the King to move, he had to get to Brenna.

At the edge of the forest, he paused for only a moment to take in the sight of the fortress that stood at the centre of Gorm's kingdom. He could see no sign of Ragnar. He had to put his faith in the huscarl, and the gods, that he had made it inside and found his wife and daughter. Mayhap Ragnar had taken out any warrior standing guard.

With sword drawn and heart in his mouth, Vali ran straight for the open gate. Finding no evidence of guards, he moved inside the first wall.

"What is this place?" he muttered, finding the second wall. He followed the road inside, ever watchful for signs of life.

As he came to the crossroad, the silence was suddenly shattered by galloping hooves. Pressing himself against the wall of a longhouse, he saw three riders approach at speed. The first man he recognised instantly.

"Ivar!" he roared, stepping out of the shadow. Given the chance, he would not let the níðingr keep betraying Brenna.

The horses passed him in a flurry of dust. Just as he thought he'd missed his chance, the horses drew to a halt at the first gate. After a brief interaction, the lead horse cantered back in his direction as the other two continued out of the fortress.

Vali grinned, sheathing his sword in favour of his axe. *This time, Ivar, you will not talk your way out of the fate you deserve.*

"I see you've crawled out from whatever rock you've been hiding under, Vali Hrolfsson." Ivar slid from his horse, slapping its backside to move the animal out of the way.

"You're a traitor."

"Am I? I don't believe Gorm sees me that way." Ivar sneered, withdrawing his sword.

He doesn't even deny it. Vali swivelled the axe in his hand, itching for his blade to taste blood.

"Where is Brenna?"

"She's with her father - her real father," he grinned, "and the reunion looks to be a happy one."

"I've never believed a word that came from your lying mouth, and I don't intend to start now."

Ivar rolled his eyes. "I've had enough of you, slápr. Your only worth was in distracting Brenna as her bedfellow, and that is of little value now she is with her true father." He raised his sword.

Vali swung his axe, connecting with Ivar's sword. The níðingr had decent reflexes. He pushed back, narrowing his eyes on his opponent. He stepped forward, then to the side, freeing his axe and taking a swipe at his arm, only to be blocked again.

"You've grown weak, playing messenger boy for your woman on the sea," snarled Ivar.

Vali growled, then hacked with his axe three times, finding only his sword but managing to drive him back.

Ivar laughed. "Temper, temper."

He bristled, and swung harder at the níðingr.

Ivar ducked then thrust his sword, getting close enough to scratch his leather breastplate. The sword sliced dangerously close to Vali's thigh, only just blocking the attack with his axe. Ivar came at him again and again, and Vali lost all the ground he'd forced from him.

His breathing came in fits and starts. Thor's hammer, what was wrong with him? He'd let the níðingr get inside his head.

Vali bellowed, pivoting to avoid the sword, then hefted his axe down from over his head. Ivar had to reach high to block the blade, exposing his belly. Vali stabbed the broad side of his axe into his gut, knocking the wind from him. As Ivar stumbled back, Vali swung his axe again, slicing his upper arm.

"That's more like it," said Ivar. "Now I feel like I'm fighting a real warrior."

He would show him a warrior. Vali hacked at the wounded arm once more. Ivar blocked the move.

"Too obvious."

"You talk too much." Vali came at him again.

Ivar chuckled as he blocked all of Vali's efforts.

Frustration and anger fused as the clarity he was used to in battle deserted him. He could not feel the presence of his ancestors or the gods with him. He was alone. But he could not allow this man to defeat him. Ivar could not win. Who would watch out for Brenna, especially when she refused to see what was right in front of her?

He withdrew his sword. Gripping both weapons, he thrust and jabbed, swung and sliced. Ivar deflected everything he threw at him, the smirk never leaving his face. He lunged forward, trying to get under the reach of Ivar's sword, only to feel the blade graze his knuckles and knock his own sword from his hand.

Streð mik! The cut on his hand stung, though not as much as his pride at losing his weapon. Ivar's sword came at him again and he only just blocked it with his axe from taking his head off.

"This has been fun, but I must get back to the battlefield. Gorm has ordered King Aric taken prisoner."

"You'll never take Aric." Vali began to move to his right, buying some time to recover. If Ivar had meant to tire him, he'd succeeded.

"Your King was as easy to fool as your Valkyrie," said Ivar.

The two of them moved in a circle, eyeing each other.

"You underestimate Brenna."

"And you are blinded by lust."

Vali grimaced. He wasn't blinded by anything. "I've always seen you clearly enough."

"Ja, that is true," Ivar chuckled again. "But no one takes you seriously, Vali. Your place was in the Jarl's bed, not her council."

He thrust his sword at the hand holding the axe, slicing the tops of Vali's fingers open. Ivar pulled the weapon up under the blade and jerked the axe free.

He was disarmed! Not since he was a boy had he suffered such an indignity. Vali reached for his dagger,

knowing he would need to get close enough to Ivar to use it
- a feat he'd not managed so far.

The men stood still. Vali had his back to the road leading
to the main entrance.

"You really believe Odin wants you in his Golden Hall?"
sneered Ivar, keeping his sword levelled at Vali's throat.

"My ancestors wait for me in Valhalla," he replied with a
steady voice. If his time had come, he would go to the All-
father as a warrior, not a coward. He raised his chin, glaring
at the man who would end his life.

"I doubt you could say the same, Ivar."

Brenna?

A sword exited Ivar's chest, pushing blood and gore
through leather. He looked down at the blade. When he
raised his head once more, blood gurgled and dripped from
his mouth. The sword withdrew and Ivar fell to his knees,
then face down on the ground.

Standing before him, bloodied sword in hand, was his
Valkyrie.

25

*V*ali moved to her side. "Brenna-"

"We don't have much time." He saw a hint of guilt in her eyes. "Did Ivar send anyone out to the battle?"

Vali explained what had transpired.

"We need to move Ivar's body," she said, sheathing her sword.

Vali retrieved his own weapons, before grabbing one of Ivar's arms and helping drag his corpse into the shadow of the longhouse. Facedown and without his shield, the dead man could be anybody.

"Where is Gorm?" he asked.

Brenna began moving back in the direction she'd appeared from.

"Dead," she threw over her shoulder.

Dead? One hundred questions sprang to mind.

"And Ragnar? Hertha?"

"They are alive. Come, we must return to them."

Vali shook himself from his daze and followed her. "Thank-"

Brenna stopped short, turning to face him. "Please

don't." The expression on her face pleaded with him to not say the words. "There is much we need to talk about, but not now."

He swallowed his discomfort. There were more pressing matters to attend to, as always.

Turning on her heel, Brenna continued on to the great hall.

Vali took in the impressive structure, following in her wake. Once inside, Brenna barred the door behind them. Vali glanced around. More than the grandeur, it was the stillness that struck him. No servants scurried in the shadows, noble families did not lounge around the fire pit as they did in Aric's hall, nor were there women weaving or men arguing.

"Come," said Brenna. She moved past the ornately carved throne, holding back the curtain to reveal a staircase. He followed her up the stairs into the sleeping quarters. At the end of the room was a grisly sight.

"Vali!" said Ragnar, leaving his wife's side to greet him.

The older man clapped him on both arms, then pulled him in for a bear hug. "I am pleased to see you!"

"And you," replied Vali, his eyes stayed focused on Hertha and the long spear she held in her hands. Blood still dripped a little from the lifeless head of Gorm that was spiked on top. His body lay off to the side.

"Ivar is dead, but he managed to send messengers with Gorm's command." Brenna's brisk tone snapped his attention back to her.

"Vali, did you speak with Aric?" asked Ragnar.

"Nei, I sent Eric and Snorri."

"The messengers may have been intercepted," said Hertha.

"It's possible," agreed Brenna.

Vali's head spun as the conversation shifted rapidly away from his comprehension.

"What," he raised his voice above the others, gesturing at the spear in Hertha's hand, "happened here?"

Brenna and Ragnar exchanged a glance, eyebrows raised. Hertha stepped forward. "This," she motioned to her macabre sceptre, "is a gift courtesy of my daughter and husband."

"How..."

"I did what I had too," said Brenna.

Vali looked at her. The wound on her arm had bled through the strips binding it; the cut on her face would leave a scar. She was battered and bloodied, yet she stood tall and strong. The image of Ragnar in strength and of Hertha in grace. A true Valkyrie. His lips twitched into a smile as he inclined his head to her.

Galloping hooves broke the silence, the rumble turning to thunder as they turned into the square beneath the balcony. Brenna moved quickly to the edge of the wall, peering outside. Her body slumped, her relief palpable.

"It is Eric."

"Vali?" boomed Eric from below. "Ragnar?"

He moved to the open space at the same time as Brenna. Eric and a dozen men sat on horseback. Relief coursed through him.

"Eric, all is well," he called.

"Praise the gods!"

"Is King Aric on his way?" asked Brenna.

Eric grinned and held his arms open. "Everyone is on their way!"

. . .

VALI VOLUNTEERED to go back down to the hall and open the doors for Eric and his men. In truth, he needed a moment to consider all that had occurred. While his suspicions of Ivar had been proven correct, Brenna had defeated both him and Gorm despite his warnings. Had he been wrong to not believe that she would eventually see the betrayal and right those wrongs?

The gods had long ago prophesied Brenna's fate was to rule, and the Seer had said their fates were intertwined. Mayhap he had misunderstood the role he was to play? Trade envoy. Warrior. Lover. Would there ever be more?

He shook the thoughts from his head, welcoming the warriors of Birca into the great hall of Gyldarhagi. The hall of Brenna's ancestors.

Following Brenna's instructions, the throne was removed from the dais and placed near the doors, where Gorm's headless corpse was sat and bound into position with ropes. Gorm's golden circlet and double-headed axe lay at his feet.

Vali and Eric closed the doors behind them and went to greet Aric and his jarls as they began to arrive with their armies into the square. Word quickly spread of King Aric's great victory in sending many of Gorm's army to Valhalla. Dozens more had slunk away in search of a more profitable and victorious cause, most likely.

A hush fell over the gathered warriors as Brenna appeared on the balcony above.

"King Aric," her voice echoed across the rows of Vikings, "I am overjoyed to see that with the strength of Thor, the bravery of Tyr and the cunning of Odin, you have led our armies to your greatest victory."

A cheer went up. Sitting atop his horse, Aric bowed his head, accepting the tribute.

Vali saw the satisfied smile on the King's face.

"In defeating Gorm, you have returned the throne of Gyldarhagi to its rightful heir." Brenna turned to look behind her.

Hertha moved into sight, holding the spiked head of Gorm. Ragnar appeared, a step behind her.

"All hail Ingrid, Queen of Gyldarghagi!" called Brenna.

"Hail Queen Ingrid!"

"Hail Queen Ingrid!"

The roar of approval swept across the square like an incoming tide, swallowing all in its wake. Vali joined the chant, but refrained from adding his own cry to the wave of noise. He was pleased with the outcome, with Gorm's defeat. The alternative would have meant death for many of his friends and countrymen. But his place in Birca seemed... uncertain. As did his place in Brenna's life. She'd proven she did not need his advice, or even his sword.

The noise began to abate. Hertha was calling for quiet.

"Friends and allies, the gods are truly with us this day."

The crowd agreed with more cheering and foot stomping. Hertha held her hand up for silence. The other hand still held the gruesome sceptre.

"A lifetime has passed before this day arrived," Hertha continued. "At last, the deaths of my Father, King Haldor, and my Mother, Queen Runa, have been avenged by their granddaughter."

She turned to Brenna. "My daughter. Jarl Brenna of Birca; the Princess of Gyldarhagi."

The roar drowned Vali once more. He was glad of their adulation of Brenna; she deserved it.

When the noise receded, Hertha spoke again.

"Of course, none of this would be possible without the actions of one man."

Even from his position in the square, Vali could see

Hertha's eyes glistening. "Ragnar Ericsson rescued me from the beast all these summers ago. He helped me heal with his love and his strength. He kept me safe. He kept our daughter safe by teaching her to fight."

Heads nodded in the crowd.

"And today, he laid the head of my enemy at my feet."

Murmurs began to rise in volume.

"I thank the gods every day for bringing Ragnar to me."

Hertha held her hand out to Ragnar. He stepped forward to stand beside her, nodding in acknowledgement of her praise.

"Hail Ragnar!" cried a voice from the crowd.

"Hail Ragnar!"

Vali watched on as Hertha and Ragnar gazed into each other's eyes. A chasm slowly opening in his gut.

"Ragnar has been loyal to King Aric all these years, and I know that loyalty stands even now," said Hertha. "Which is why I could not ask him to rule beside me, here in Gyldarhagi."

Vali stood up straighter. What was Hertha planning?

"I thank all of you who answered the call to fight in my name."

Vali glanced at Aric. The frown on the King's face suggested he was as unsure as to what was happening as well.

"And I believe you will support my decision to hand the crown of Gyldarhagi into the capable hands of my heir."

The crowd inhaled a collective gasp.

"My daughter - Brenna, the Valkyrie of Birca; and now the Queen of Gyldarhagi!"

Vali's eyes flew to Brenna. It was clear she had not known what her mother was planning. She stared, open mouthed at Hertha.

"All hail Queen Brenna!" boomed Ragnar.

"All hail Queen Brenna." Hertha joined him.

Slowly, Brenna faced the crowd below as they added their voices to the chant. Eventually, her eyes came to rest on his.

Vali bowed his head to her.

Mayhap, she had no need of him at all. He'd loved her from afar for many seasons, he could do it again if that is what the gods had planned for him.

Hail Queen Brenna!

26

*B*renna ordered the doors to the great hall be opened and Gorm's body, bound to his throne, carried outside the fortress. Hertha relinquished his spiked head, and once reunited with the body in the field outside of the city, they were set on fire and left to burn. Odin and his Valkyries would determine if the warlord was worthy of Valhalla.

She sent teams of warriors into the longhouses, where they found the people of Gyldarhagi locked inside. They were starving and most were broken in spirit; too afraid to cry out for help when they heard Aric's armies enter the fortress.

Gorm's thralls were found in chains, cowering behind the great hall. When they heard of Gorm's demise, many ran to the field to witness the tyrant burn to ash. Hertha did her best to give comfort with her words and a promise of better days to come, introducing Brenna as her heir and their new Queen. No mention was made of Gorm's role in her conception.

At Brenna's request, servants who'd travelled with King

Aric and his jarls set about finding cows to slaughter and chickens to roast. The kitchen was well stocked with root vegetables and bread. A large supply of ale and mead was found and brought out for all to share.

"King Aric," Brenna approached the King. "Would you lead the sacrifice to the gods for your victory?"

He looked her up and down. "This is now your kingdom, is it not?"

"Ja, sire. But it is your army that led to this victory."

Brenna may be new to her title, but she knew enough of Aric to understand his ego must be stroked if she wanted to maintain a friendly alliance.

"And I would like the gothi to consult the gods before the ritual to anoint me as Queen is performed. I want peace for Gyldarhagi and I would ensure the gods accept my mother's decision to pass the crown to me before it is done." She wanted Aric to have no doubts as to the legitimacy of her claim to the throne.

Aric narrowed his gaze. "A wise decision, *Jarl* Brenna."

Her shoulders tensed, but she did not challenge the King. She did not need his blessing to be Queen of this land. It was hers by birthright; she was sure the gods would agree.

Brenna gave directions to the servants to prepare for the ritual, and then the feast, to celebrate their victory. Everyone would eat well tonight. And every night after, if she had her way.

A makeshift camp had been created between the two walls of the fortress. The Jarls and their hersirs were examining the fortifications with great interest. The ringed fortress was like nothing they'd ever seen and they were eager to learn its secrets.

One of the quadrants within the walls had been set aside to bring the wounded for care. Gorm's thralls had been instructed to strip the great hall of its furs and skins, and distribute them to the people of Gyldarhagi. Although the blood would be scrubbed clean and all traces of Gorm removed, Brenna had no intention of sleeping in the private quarters until she had renewed every surface and alcove.

She busied herself with these tasks to avoid facing her conscience. She'd not believed Vali; not even entertained his perspective. How could he ever forgive her? How could she ever forgive herself?

SHE FOUND her mother in a newly erected tent, fit for a queen. She sank onto the bench beside her, resting her head on Hertha's shoulder. Her mother pulled her hand onto her lap, lacing their fingers together.

"Thank you, Brenna," she whispered into her hair. "Thank you for saving me. Again."

She lifted her head. "Again?"

"When I realised I was pregnant with you, I found the will to live again."

Brenna leaned her forehead against her mother's. "I'm sorry I doubted your reasons for not telling me."

Hertha shook her head. "Let us not dwell in the past any longer." Taking Brenna's face in her hands, she examined the dried blood on Brenna's cheek.

Brenna smiled and let her mother remove her battle armour after calling for a bucket of warm water and fresh linens. Hertha washed the blood and sweat from her body, murmuring endearments to her, as she'd done when Brenna was a child and had scraped her knee.

The water stung when it touched the wound on her arm.

"The cut is deep, but I cannot see the bone," said Hertha. She sent a servant to find her a poultice of willow tree bark and ribwort while she turned her attention to Brenna's cheek.

"The poultice will work for this as well." Hertha gently rubbed the wet linen into the cut. "But you will always have a reminder of this day."

Brenna began to smile, relaxing the muscles as the sting took hold. "What is one more scar to add to the collection?"

"In any case, I don't think Vali will mind."

Sadness washed over her, pinching her heart. She'd pushed him so far away.

"Brenna, what is it?"

She took a breath, surprised to find it shaking. Brenna had locked her thoughts and feelings over her last exchange with Vali away deep inside. It was wrapped up in guilt and shame.

"I'm not sure Vali will want me at all."

Hertha lowered her hands from Brenna's face, placing them on her daughter's leg.

"Mother, I fear I've pushed him too far this time." Tears pricked the back of her eyes.

Her mother waited, silently.

"I have not treated him well." A tear escaped, sliding down her cheek. "At first, it was easy to blame others for my choices. But in truth, I have always done what I believed was best." She looked up into her mother's eyes. "For me."

Hertha dabbed the tears that fell with abandon down her face.

"I've always known Vali loves me," she whispered, hanging her head. "But he has had many reasons to doubt my love for him."

Placing a finger beneath her chin, Hertha lifted her face. "Do you love him?"

Brenna nodded. "I do."

"Then go to him. Tell him you love him and vow that he will never have cause to doubt your love again."

She clasped her hands together, if only it were that easy.

"Is love enough?"

Hertha looked at her, patience etched into her face. "What do you mean?"

"I am Jarl, nei! You made me Queen today."

She shook her head. "I have never even thought to share that burden with Vali." Shame began to burn inside her. "I don't know how to."

"Oh Brenna," whispered her mother, pulling her against her shoulder. "I cannot tell you how to love, or how to rule. But I have learnt, through many years with your father, that much can be achieved when you give yourself over to fate and the gods. Trust them to guide you."

The gods had always guided her in her quest to rule. Was it possible she'd been asking them the wrong questions? She sank into her mother's embrace, letting her hold her up as she crumbled on the inside. Even if she knew how, would it be too late to make things right with Vali?

27

*T*he great hall of Gyldarhagi overflowed. Warriors and townspeople sat shoulder to shoulder as the ale flowed. Outside, the square was just as full. Gyldarhagi and her fortress had been transformed from a silent prison to a place of joy and victory.

The line of people wanting to see the saviours of Gyldarhagi up close was never-ending. Hertha, or Ingrid as the people called her, Ragnar and Brenna barely swallowed a morsel of food, so busy were they accepting the blessings of those who had been set free by the death of Gorm. King Aric was kept equally occupied; hailed as a mighty warrior and hero.

Brenna had searched for Vali at the sacrifice and then again as she entered the great hall, to no avail. She kept her smile in place, despite the heavy weight of wretchedness that had settled in her belly. His absence felt like a thousand cuts upon her skin.

A warmth whispered passed her cheek, as familiar as it was comforting. Unseen fingertips lifted her chin, its touch sending light and strength into the dark and despair that had filled her core.

Across the room, leaning against a pillar, was Vali. She watched as he straightened his stance, then looked directly at her. An imperceptible connection held them both. Her smile was timid and unsure; he raised a corner of his mouth.

The gifted light and strength inside pulled her to her feet. A weighted hush rolled out, quieting the crowd.

What am I to say?

Speak your truth, came the whispered reply.

"Friends, allies," her smile grew. "Family. I stand before you, in the hall of my ancestors. This day was fated by the gods long ago, and now it has come to pass."

She reached deeper inside herself, searching for the words to bring her truth into the light. "I have always trusted the gods to guide my path, and they have never failed me. But as we all know, our own actions shape our destiny. We cannot rely on the gods alone to determine our fate. Those who are not worthy, will have their fate rewritten."

She looked out at the faces in the hall. Some she knew, many she didn't. All of them focused on her as she spoke.

"Those who allow power and wealth to be their only motivation, will find the gods no longer smile on them, despite their skill on the battlefield or the grandness of their hall."

She gestured around her as she spoke, not needing to name the tyrant that had ruled this land for so long. Yet the irony was not lost on her.

"Those that let their people starve while they grow fat on plunder, will lose the favour of the gods. And those that close their ears to the sage advice of those that know them best, risk losing sight of what is most important."

Heads nodded. She took a breath, her gaze settling on Vali once more. "I do not know if we could have avoided the bloodshed of battle today, and I will never know. I did not listen to the one person who could see past the politics of power and position. The one person who would never betray me."

Every person and thing faded into the background until Vali was all she could see. She let the words tumble forth, without censor.

"I am sorry I would not listen to you, Vali. Your counsel was never self-serving and I was wrong to doubt your intentions."

His expression did not change. She could not read him, fearing she was too late with her apology.

"You have always been loyal to King Aric, to Birca... and to me. Even when I did not deserve it. But I vow to you, from this day forward, I will not dismiss your loyalty or your counsel again."

28

*T*he feast continued well into the night, and the cavalcade of well-wishers was never-ending. Finally, Brenna was able to slip away with Hertha and Ragnar through the kitchen, bypassing the square. They followed the road to the outer ring, where the tents had been set up. Brenna did not want to disrupt the feasting, but she could not sleep in the private quarters. Not yet.

As they reached the tent where Ragnar and Hertha would sleep, Brenna paused. "I am sorry for my reaction in Birca, when you told me the truth of my parentage," she said quietly.

"You do not need to apologise, Brenna," said Hertha. "It was a shock."

"Be that as it may," she said. "It changes nothing. I am the daughter of Ragnar Eriksson and Hertha. That is who I will always be."

As Ragnar squeezed her shoulder, she could see the tears in his eyes.

Hertha pulled in close. "You did the right thing, apologising to Vali," she whispered. "All will be well, Daughter."

Brenna hugged her mother. She wanted to believe, with all her heart, that Hertha was correct.

She left her parents at their tent, and trudged off to hers. She'd not seen Vali since she'd apologised. At least he'd heard her say she was wrong; that she was sorry.

The wounds on her arm and face throbbed and her body ached from the battle. But most of all, her heart felt as though it had been battered, and by her own hand. Sighing, she pulled back the opening of her tent and hoped the gods would grant her the small mercy of sleep.

A fire burned in a dugout pit, warming the space and casting a low light. It took her eyes a moment to adjust and realise she was not alone. She inhaled a sharp intake of breath.

Vali.

He looked as he always did: tall and strong and handsome. His hands were lightly bandaged and she wondered briefly who had tended to his wounds. She forced herself to look into his eyes, terrified of what she might find there. Vali was a man of honour; he would not just walk away.

But he looked back at her, his expression unchanged. She saw love and respect, strength and determination. Was she dreaming?

"I didn't think they'd ever let you go," he said softly.

"We snuck out the back."

He smiled. "I've been waiting for you. I-"

"Nei, there's more." She rushed forward, stopping when she saw the confusion on his face. "I mean, there is more I need to say. Please?"

He nodded.

She took a breath to steady the frantic beating of her heart. "You've always loved me, Vali. And I have taken that for granted." She held up her hand when he opened his mouth to speak.

"Please, I must say this." She could not bear another moment to pass without him knowing the truth.

"I have made choices, thinking only of myself, of my own burden, knowing those choices would hurt you, and push you aside.

"You have sacrificed and made changes, all to be with me. And now I fear I have used up all the love you had for me." She swallowed back the tears that threatened to overwhelm her.

"I love you, Vali. I love you with all my heart and soul. I'm sorry that I did not make sure to tell you this every day that I've known you." Her legs threatened to give out from under her.

"Brenna, I've always known that you love me."

"How?" she shook her head. How could he know after the way she'd treated him?

There was no anger or hurt hidden in his eyes. His smile was soft and gentle. "Because you always come back to me."

They moved towards each other, his mouth claiming hers and his touch healing her bruised heart. She held him tighter, unable to get close enough. This time, she would not let him go. She would never leave him again.

She pulled back from the kiss, her mind clear and made up.

"Vali, you once asked me to marry you."

"I did-'

"And I said that I loved you, but that had to be enough."

Doubt crept into his eyes.

"It's not enough for me anymore," she whispered.

"What do you mean?"

"Vali Hrolfsson, will you marry me?"

His grin lit up his entire face. "My Valkyrie, I thought you would never ask."

He swept her up into his arms, spinning her around.

Her lips found his again. She'd almost lost herself completely when she felt a familiar breeze tickle the back of her neck. Once more, she pulled away from his kiss.

"I didn't actually hear you agree to marry me?"

"Well," said Vali, placing her feet back on the ground. A frown creased his brow and he took a step back. "It is an interesting proposal. Let me think on it."

"Vali!" She slapped his arm.

"Alright!" A cheeky smile erased the frown. "I accept!"

"Thank the gods," she said.

The tent filled with a joyful energy. Brenna swore she could hear laughter on the wind that whispered around them before disappearing into the night.

Vali picked her up in his arms and carried her to the makeshift bed. Laying her down, he unlaced her boots and slipped them off, doing the same with his own.

She watched as he pulled his shirt over his head, unlaced his trousers and pushed them down his hips. A deep yearning grew inside of her. A need to have him close, to feel him inside her. She reached for him as he lay beside her, her hands roaming the hard muscle of his chest and arms.

He traced the contour of her jaw, then her lips with the tip of his finger. They kissed, slowly, softly. The ties of her tunic came loose in his hands, working the fabric down her shoulders.

"Now it's my turn," he whispered against her neck.

"Your turn?"

"To show you how much I love you."

A sigh escaped her lips as he feathered kisses along her collarbone. Her tunic fell to her belly. His hands, calloused from the sea and battle, gently palmed her breasts. She arched her back as his mouth found her nipple, shivering with the pleasure from his tongue flicking back and forth.

He moved down her body, bringing her clothing with him. She parted her legs to allow his fingers to stroke her womanhood, teasing her open with slow, firm movements. Sparks of desire shot through her belly. He dropped his head between her legs, kissing and licking her slick, wet mound.

She brought her knees up, granting him greater access. He kept the same rhythm, driving her slowly to the edge of the abyss. As she was about to tip over, he snaked his way up her body. She could taste her own sweet saltiness on his mouth, running her tongue over his lips for more.

He pushed himself inside her, slowly, until he filled every part of her. His lips left hers, his clear blue eyes holding her own as he moved in and out. Wrapping her legs around his waist, she rose to meet him as his thrusts increased his pace. Ecstasy took hold, squeezing her from the inside out. She closed her eyes.

"Look at me!" he commanded in soft tones.

She opened her eyes, only to drown in his. They clung to each other as they lost control, their voices crying out in unison.

Vali lay down on his back, drawing her into his arms. His heart galloped in his chest against her ear, matching her own heartbeat.

This was where she belonged - in the arms of the man who'd always loved her. This was where she knew who she was. No matter the fate bestowed on her by the gods, Brenna knew her destiny lay with Vali. Always.

The End.

COMING SOON

THE VALKYRIE QUEEN

BOOK 3 - THE VALKYRIE OF BIRCA SERIES

PROLOGUE

*G*yldarhagi AD 821, Yuletide - four months after Gorm's defeat.

The night was cold and clear and the sky was full. The stars had been joined by the light of the Valkyries called to be honoured on this, the eleventh night of Yule. The gothi of Gyldarhagi had come down from their sanctuary in the mountains, once they'd been liberated from Gorm's harsh rule. It was the elder gothi, Solfrid who had foreseen the return of King Hador's lineage, in the shape of a Valkyrie.

Brenna followed the trail of her breath, her body tingling all over. The drums beat a slow rhythm as she and her women made their way to the top of the cliffs that overlooked the fjord and the docks of her new kingdom. The warriors of Birca formed a guard of honour, and the people of Gyldarhagi gathered along the docks and the banks of the fjord.

This was not her first wedding, but it was the only marriage she'd pursued with her heart and her head. The only union in which love was present. By the end of this night, Brenna and Vali would be crowned Queen and King of Gyldarhagi. The prophecy that had haunted her since childhood would be fulfilled. Despite the cold, she felt warmth radiating from within as she smiled at each of the well-wishers.

Beneath her furs, her long red gown hugged her body. Gold necklaces glittered around her throat and chest. Her blonde hair had been intricately braided against her head, with deep burgundy and salmon-pink amaryllis blooms woven into a half crown around the back of her hair. Tonight, she felt like a queen; Vali's Queen.

He waited for her at the top of the cliff. His hair was shaved at the sides, highlighting the inked warrior wolf above his left temple, and the newer markings depicting his strength in battle, loyalty and status. The rest was tied back into a long braid that fell down his back. His beard was knotted below his chin, and his blue eyes twinkled with anticipation as she approached. His broad frame was clad in a deep brown leather tunic and arm bracers, over black trousers. His fur wrapped around his shoulders, held together with a gold chain that matched the buckle on his belt.

Her breath hitches and her heart skipped a beat as she watched him, taking in every part of him. He looked like a king. He was her king.

She reached the summit and the drums quit abruptly, their hum fading into the night, leaving only the rapid beat of her own heart in their wake. Ragnar and Frode stood with Vali, along with his brother-in-law, Hagen. Hertha kissed her cheek as Ragnar joined them. Nissa and Vali's mother and sisters went to stand with their men, leaving Gita by her side. Not far from the bridal party, all of their important guests had gathered, including King Aric and Queen Yvla.

"People of Gyldarhagi." The voice of Solfrid rang out across the cliff and down onto the beach. "We are gathered here, as we once did so many moons ago to witness the marriage of King Haldor and Queen Runa. This night, we will bear witness to the marriage of their granddaughter, Brenna, daughter of Ingrid and Ragnar to Vali, son of Hrolf and Eira.

Brenna looked up into Vali's eyes. His smile brightened his whole face and she longed to pull him close and press her lips to his. She returned his grin.

"This Yuletide we have celebrated many blessings from the gods," Solfrid continued. "We have honoured Odin, Njord, and Freyr for victory in battle and good harvests with sacrifices and feasting. And it is right that on this night, when we honour the Valkyries, that Vali and Brenna are joined as husband and wife."

Vali reached for her hand and squeezed her fingers. Tiny winged horses galloped around her stomach.

"We ask the gods to bless the love between Vali and Brenna. May it keep you both, and protect you in times of happiness and sadness."

A horse, a goat and a cow were led to the clearing just behind the bridal party closest to the fortress below. Solfrid moved into the clearing, taking the long, silver dagger presented to her by one of the younger gothi. An altar built from large, smooth stones held carved figures of the gods. Below, wooden bowls waited to catch the blood.

"Mighty Thor, may your courage and strength guide Vali and Brenna in all they do."

Solfrid whispered into the ear of the horse, then ran the

blade across its throat. The horse fell to its knees, its blood rushing over the altar and into the first bowl.

"Beautiful Frigga, goddess of love and marriage, bless this union and protect their home."

Again, Solfrid whispered into the ear of the goat before drawing her blade across its throat.

"Freya, we honour you with this sacrifice and ask that you bless this couple with many strong sons and daughters."

The ritual was repeated with the cow.

Solfrid dipped her fingers into each of the bowls then, returning to Brenna and Vali, traced the rune symbolising a happy marriage and family onto each of their foreheads. The younger gothi used a switch to splatter the sacred blood over those gathered at the top of the summit.

From behind her, Hertha stepped forward and placed the sword of her father, King Haldor, into Brenna's hands. She held the blade upright, its gilt and pommel interlaid with gold, so Ragnar could place a ring on its point.

Eira, in turn, handed Vali his father's sword. His eyes glistened with tears as he held the heavy weapon. His father meant everything to Vali, and he'd missed him since his death when he was a boy. Eira also placed a golden ring on its point before caressing her son's cheek, then stepping back.

They faced each other, Brenna's heart felt so full she thought it must surely burst. They crossed their swords and waited for Solfrid to begin.

"Vali, do you swear before the gods on this day that you want to take this woman as your wife?"

"I swear by Odin and Frigga," said Vali. He took the ring from his sword and placed it on her finger. "When Ragnarok comes and the sun is dashed from the sky." He pushed the ring into place. "When the mountains crumble into the sea, my love for you will remain, my Valkyrie."

Tears of joy pricked the back of her eyes.

"Brenna, do you swear before the gods on this day that you want to take this man as your husband?"

"I swear by Odin and Frigga," she said, reaching for the ring on her sword. "May Odin give us knowledge on our way to come, may Thor bless our union with strength and courage, may Loki never deny us laughter." She pushed the ring onto his finger. "In this life and the next, my heart will never deny you."

"Allfather, Odin his holy name. Ragnarok will come, his destiny must be fulfilled. On Midgard and in Asgard may Odin's will guide us," said Solfrid.

"Brenna, I give you the sword of my father to keep for our sons and daughters, so they may know where they come from."

"Vali, I gave you the sword of my grandfather. Now united, may we will always have the protection of our ancestors."

They slid the swords into their belts.

"In the sight of the Valkyrie's, may Frigga bless this union," declared Solfrid. "Vali, you may kiss your bride."

The kiss was as slow and deep as the cheers of their well wishers was loud. She never wanted the moment to end, but there was one more important task to complete before the feast could begin.

Vali clasped her hand in his, leaning close to whisper in her ear. "You look beautiful, wife."

His breath beneath her ear sent shivers of warmth across her body. "And you look very handsome, husband."

Their families descended on them, with congratulations and blessings. Warriors and farmers, friends and strangers called their blessings as they made their way down the cliff and back into the fortress of Gyldarghagi.

Inside the quadrant that housed the Great Hall, the square had been prepared for the crowning of Brenna and Vali as the royal rulers. The drums beat again, heralding their entrance to the square. The gothi led them to a raised dais that held two newly carved chairs; the new thrones of Gyldargagi. Brenna's throne had the head and wings of a Valkyrie's horse carved into the back, standing tall over the seat. Vali's throne had two beautiful dragon heads in homage to his love of the sea.

Brenna and Vali took their seats, looking out across the square. Hundreds of people crowded into the space, lit with large fire pits at every corner and in the middle of the square. At the front of the crowd stood their families and King Aric and Queen Yvla. Two of Aric's jarls from the north had returned to Gyldargahi for Yuletide and the wedding. Jarl Ingolf brought his wife Oda and their young sons. Jarl Gleb and his wife Dagrun stood with their son and daughter.

The four Jarls of Gyldarhagi had been Gorm's men. Those that had not died in battle, had been executed in the days that followed victory. Brenna and Vali had traveled to all of the jarldoms and met with the elders and warriors loyal to the true heir, rounding up any who had served Gorm.

In Skapta and Kalda, Brenna had found relatives of the Jarls who ruled during Haldor's time. Jarl Magnus and his wife Aslaug had left their children in the care of family to join the royal couple. Jarl Trygve of Kalda and his hersirs stood with them. Jarl Arvid of Mydalsa had left his wife Signy and their new babe at home. His people had nominated Arvid unopposed for the role.

In Fiska, Jarl Erling had claimed the role by right of marriage. His wife was Idonea of Uppsala and one day, he would be Jarl of the holy city. With his father-in-law in good health, Erling felt he was the right person to rule Fiska. With no other candidates presenting themselves, Brenna and Vali had appointed Erling, despite the trepidation that lurked deep within her.

"The gods had long whispered of the return of the rightful heir to this throne. They whispered that Odin would send his most prized Valkyrie to free this land of hate and treachery," Solfrid, having changed from her blue gown to a long, white tunic, began.

"And so it came to pass. The Valkyrie and her Warrior defeated the Usurper of Gyldarhagi. Tonight, we gather before the gods to see them crowned as our Queen and King."

Brenna took a deep breath. Her giddy happiness at wedding Vali remained, but it sat comfortably next to a deep sense of calm. Along with her family and allies, she felt the presence of her ancestors. Their presence must have long haunted Gorm during the many seasons of his rule, for Brenna felt them all around, especially in their hall. It was little wonder he built this great fortress to protect his interests while he went raiding. She suspected he never felt this place was truly his own.

Her mother stepped forward, playing her role as the Princess Ingrid of Gyldarhagi. Hertha never wanted to sit on her father's throne, but as his heir, she would ensure the crown was placed on her daughter's head.

"Brenna, Daughter of Ingrid and Ragnar, Granddaughter of Haldor and Runa," said Solfrid. "Do you swear by the gods, and to all gathered here before you, to protect

Gyldarhagi and all its people, to be a just and fair ruler, and to protect and stand by your chosen Jarls?"

Her eyes swept the crowd, feeling their love and support flowing to her.

"I swear by Odin and all the gods, that I will."

Hertha took the crown her own mother had worn offered to her by a young gothi, and stepped in front of Brenna. She smiled down at her daughter.

"With the blessings of the gods, I crown you Brenna, Queen of Gyldarhagi."

The crown felt sturdy upon her head. Hope and honour flooded her senses.

"All Hail Queen Brenna!"

"Hail Queen Brenna," repeated the crowd. "Hail Queen Brenna."

Solfrid turned to Vali and repeated the same question to him. She placed her hand over his as he swore to the gods he would be King and protector of Gyldarhagi.

Again, Hertha accepted the crown handed to her. It was the crown of her father.

"With the blessings of the gods, I crown you Vali, King of Gyldarhagi."

"All Hail King Vali!"

"Hail King Vali!"

They raised themselves from their thrones, accepting the cheers of their people as the musicians started to play a merry jig. A year ago, Brenna could not have foreseen that she would be standing here, Jarl of Birca, Queen of Gyldarhagi, and married to the man she'd always loved. Her ancestors' scars had been healed and she'd fulfilled their destiny - her destiny.

But where happiness had reigned, a chill rushed up her spine. A warm wind whispered past her, a warning in its familiar caress. The crowd began to fade inside a veil of darkness. She tried to move, to call out, but her body refused to obey. Her chest ached as her heart thundered and all the oxygen was leeched from the air. Standing before her, was the harbinger of her foreboding.

The ancient Seer of Birca.

GLOSSARY

The Valkyrie of Birca series is set in the country now known as Sweden. Birca and some of the other towns were and are real places. Others are not. Some of the Norse terms used throughout the book will be familiar - some may not be. Many have been the subject of debate in terms of their meaning and application to the Viking age. For the purposes of this work of fiction, the following words and their interpretations are listed here.

Allfather - Odin. The god of wisdom, war, art, culture, and the dead, and the supreme deity and creator of the cosmos and humans

Asgard - The dwelling place of the gods. Asgard has 12 realms, including Valhalla.

Blood Eagle - a form of punishment and execution, where the victim's back sliced open, so their ribs and lungs could be pulled out, whilst still alive. Carrying out the Blood Eagle was seen as a human sacrifice to the Norse God Odin.

Cassia - Cinnamon.

Drakkar - A specialised warship, often with a dragon carved into the bow. Could hold over one hundred men.

Dunga - A useless and unhelpful person.

Einherjar - (Pronounced ane-hair-yah) An army of warriors who have died in battle and are brought to Valhalla by valkyries.

Faðmr - A measure of length equalling about two yards.

Fífl - (Pronounced FEEF-uhl). Stupid, fool.

Frigga - Odin's wife, Frigga, is a paragon of beauty, love, fertility and fate. She is the mighty queen of Asgard, a venerable Norse goddess, who is gifted with the power of divination, and yet, is surrounded by an air of secrecy.

Freya - One of the most sensual and passionate goddesses in Norse mythology. She is associated with much of the same qualities as Frigga: love, fertility and beauty.

Golden Hall - Another name for Valhalla.

Gothi - Minister of the gods, leads religious ceremonies. May also be healers.

Hel - The underworld where many of the dead dwell, named after the Goddess Hel who reigns there.

Hersir - A Viking military commander of about 100 men and owed allegiance to a jarl or king. They were also aspiring landowners, and, like the middle class in many feudal societies, supported the kings in their centralization of power.

Horn - The horn of a bovid (antelopes, sheep, goats, cattle, buffalo, and bison) used as a drinking vessel.

Huscarl - A member of the bodyguard or household troops of a Norse king or noble.

Jarl - Chieftain. The role of Jarl could be hereditary or bequeathed by the King.

Karvi - A small longboat, considered to be "general

purpose" ships, mainly used for fishing and trade, but occasionally commissioned for military use

Loki - The god of mischief who can shape-shift and can
take up animalistic forms.

Longboat - Specialised warship .

Miklagaard - The Great City, Constantinople.

Midgard - The realm where humans live, the Earth.

Níðingr - (NEETH-ing-uhr) villain, vile person. In Norse
mythology, there was a dragon whose name was Nidhogg
whose name probably came from this word. Nidhogg was
the dragon that gnawed at the root of Yggdrasil Tree of Life.

Ragnarok - The end of the world of gods and men.

Rassragr - Norse curse word meaning unmanly or
cowardly.

Rus - They were originally Norse people, mainly origi-
nating from Sweden, settling and ruling along the the river-
routes between the Baltic and the Black Seas from around
the 8th to 11th centuries AD.

Skal - (Pronounced skol) A toast. A Skål was a bowl that
was often filled with beer and shared among friends so the
word became a way of saying "Cheers!"

Shield maiden - Female warrior.

Sordinn - Norse curse word meaning fuck.

Streð mik - Norse curse phrase meaning fuck me.

Styrimaor - Captain of the ship; leader of the raiding
party.

Svealand - A people who gave Sweden its name (Sverige,
or Svea Rike, in Swedish, meaning "kingdom of Svea"), and
it was the nucleus from which Sweden developed politically
and culturally and later secured its independence.

Tankard - A drinking vessel consisting of a large,
roughly cylindrical, drinking cup with a single handle.

Tankards can be made of silver or pewter, wood, ceramic or leathers.

Thor - Thor is Odin's most widely-known son. He is the protector of humanity and the powerful god of thunder who wields a hammer named Mjöllnir. Among the Norse gods, he is known for his bravery, strength, healing powers and righteousness.

Ting - All free men would gather in their communities to make laws and to have conflicts ruled on. The meetings were called the Ting or Thing.

Trencher - A small plate of metal or wood, typically circular and completely flat, without the lip or raised edge of a plate.

Tyr - The god of war, a brave warrior who champions order and justice. The namesake of Tuesday, he lost his arm to Loki's ferocious offspring Fenrir, the giant wolf.

Uppsala - Home of the Temple of Uppsala and the religious epicentre of Viking culture.

Valhalla - The home of Odin and the destination of warriors slain in battle.

Valkyrie - One of Odin's twelve handmaidens who conducted the slain warriors of their choice from the battlefield to Valhalla. Valkyries were also renowned for being selfless, brave, noble, loyal and dedicated to their people.

Viking - Vikings were the seafaring Norse people from southern Scandinavia (present-day Denmark, Norway and Sweden) who from the late 8th to late 11th centuries raided, pirated, traded and settled throughout parts of Europe.

ACKNOWLEDGMENTS

One of the many upsides of writing Viking romance is that I get to read a lot of Viking romance - it's kind of mandatory! Thank you to all of the other Viking romance authors who have entertained me with their tales of pillage and plunder. The Viking Age is rich in stories, and there is no end of opportunity for interpretation and retelling.

Reading about Vikings led me to the fabulous Ree Thornton - fellow Aussie and Viking romance author. Ree and I have spent many hours talking about all things Viking. Ree was one of the first people to read *The Valkyrie's Rule* and helped me iron out some of the bigger plot tangles, ensuring the romance didn't get left behind by all the battles. She also helped guide me through the fine art of marketing and selling a Viking romance. Thanks for sharing your wisdom with me!

A big shout out to Michelle Montebello, Rania Battany, Anna Foxkirk and Davina Stone for sharing the highs and lows, and ins and outs of the indie publishing journey.

Writing and publishing a book is a major roller coaster - thank the gods for all of you!

Sara Hartland - you're an absolute diamond on the precipice of showering the night sky with all of your talented light. I love our long chats and our shared refusal to give up drinking. Thanks for cheering me up when I'm on the verge of grabbing my sword and my axe and sorting out those who have annoyed me. (Happens more often than you'd think...)

And finally, to those of you who've read my books, thank you from the bottom of my heart!

ABOUT THE AUTHOR

Australian author Tanya Nellestein writes page-turning, gut-churning Viking romance, romantic bikie thrillers and crime/mystery with a romantic angle that always includes good sex and a happily ever after - eventually.

To find out more or sign up for her newsletter, visit www.-tanyanellestein.com

To really make her day, please leave a review on Amazon, Goodreads or Bookbub.

Skal!

She won her kingdom with her sword, but to save it she will have to learn to trust her heart and her head.

Coming August 2021 on Amazon

The Valkyrie Returns

Book 4: The Valkyrie of Birca

Coming 2021/2022

Fix Your Crown

NEVER underestimate the power of a *FIERCE* woman. 13 authors have come together to write a collection of short stories that show just how strong women can be.

100% of proceeds will be donated to breast cancer support. Fix Your Crown will be available on all major e-retailers from September 28, 2021.

www.ingramcontent.com/pod-product-compliance
Lightning Source LLC
Chambersburg PA
CBHW070023120726
47909CB00003B/1039